Jordan Lake Would Be
The Ultimate Takeover.

"Does it bother you," he asked roughly, "this secret of ours? This thing between us?"

Jordan was past reason. She wanted much more of "this thing" between them, and she wanted it now.

With an effort almost too much to bear, she forced her mouth to open, to speak. "I know the score, Nick," she told him tightly. "I'm playing the game."

Sex.

Simple. Sensational. Secret.

Dear Reader,

Feuding fathers are great catalysts for romance stories. I don't recall my father ever feuding with anyone but I think most feuds involve great wealth, and I could never accuse my dad of that! What I can accuse him of is imbuing me with a love of stories. He used to tell wonderful tales of his life in the British and Australian armies in India and Korea. (I suspect he still does, but sadly, the pace of life and my inability to sit still long enough means that he doesn't get the chance very often.) As an aside, my dad is one of the few people in the world who could say he has met Mahatma Gandhi, Marilyn Monroe and Nelson Mandela.

But back to feuding fathers: Historical conflict between families gives a writer rich pickings to inflict suffering on the new generation. The hero and heroine of this book struggle with the sins of their fathers and events not of their making. But in my mind, two cranky old men will one day sit on the couch together, dangling the grandkids on their knees and telling them about the time they…

Hope you enjoy Nick and Jordan's story.

Best wishes,

Jan Colley

FRIDAY
NIGHT
MISTRESS

JAN COLLEY

Silhouette®

Desire

Published by Silhouette Books

America's Publisher of Contemporary Romance

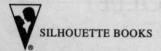

SILHOUETTE BOOKS

ISBN-13: 978-0-373-76932-2
ISBN-10:   0-373-76932-6

Recycling programs
for this product may
not exist in your area.

FRIDAY NIGHT MISTRESS

Visit Silhouette Books at www.eHarlequin.com

Printed in U.S.A.

Books by Jan Colley

Silhouette Desire

Trophy Wives #1698
Melting the Icy Tycoon #1770
Expecting a Fortune #1795
Satin & a Scandalous Affair #1861
Billionaire's Favorite Fantasy #1882
Friday Night Mistress #1932

JAN COLLEY

lives in Christchurch, New Zealand, with Les and a couple of cats. She has traveled extensively, is jack of all trades and master of none and still doesn't know what she wants to be when she grows up—as long as it's a writer. She loves rugby, family and friends, writing, sunshine, talking about writing and cats, although not necessarily in that order. E-mail her at vagabond232@yahoo.com or check out her Web site at www.jancolley.com.

Thanks for all the stories, Dad!
And thanks to Stephen Bray, our friendly family lawyer,
who let me pester him about courtroom legalese
and only charged me a chocolate fish.
And to Maureen Coffey of Havelock Sea Charters
who answered my questions about chartering a boat
in the Marlborough Sounds of New Zealand.

One

"All rise."

Spectators and participants in the Wellington High Court rose as one. Day one of the defamation case brought by Randall Thorne, founder of Thorne Financial Enterprises, against Syrius Lake had begun.

Seated behind his father in the front row of the gallery, Nick Thorne frowned as his younger brother slipped into the empty seat beside him. "You're late," Nick muttered without heat. Adam was always late, even while on holiday.

The judge bustled in and motioned for everyone to take their seats.

"Would you look at that?" Adam whispered, nudging

Nick. "Little Jordan Lake, all grown up and pretty as a picture."

Nick tilted his head and flicked a glance to his right. He'd noticed her earlier, surprised at how demure she looked with her hair tied back, wearing a white blouse and a knee-length black skirt. Everyone here would be more used to seeing her in the tabloids, partying it up with some rock star or other, her golden hair flowing and plenty of long, smooth leg on display. She was every inch the heiress, daughter of one of the richest and most flamboyant men in New Zealand.

Adam leaned in close. "I'm surprised you've never considered hooking up with her. An alliance with the Lake princess would be one way to bury this stupid hatchet that's been the bane of our lives forever."

"She's more your type than mine," Nick murmured, settling back in his seat as his father turned his head and sent him a disapproving look.

It was true. Jordan and Adam were rebels, whereas Nick was duty-driven and responsible. The brothers could almost pass as twins with their olive coloring, dark hair and brows and their father's tall, broad frame. But Adam, with his designer stubble, flashy suits and bad boy demeanor, was far removed from the quieter, more conservative Nick.

"True," Adam whispered, rubbing his chin thoughtfully, "but I live in London."

The infamous feud between Randall Thorne and Syrius Lake had tainted their whole lives, especially their late mother's, a former close friend of Syrius's wife, Elanor. Nick felt a pang of compassion for the woman sitting at the end of the row in the aisle to his right. Elanor had spent thirty years in a wheelchair because of Nick's father, all the more galling because she and his mother were once national ballroom dancing competitors and partners in their own dance studio.

"You can't help your looks, big brother," Adam went on, "but you're still not a bad catch. CEO of the biggest privately-owned finance company in New Zealand…"

"Not yet," Nick said tersely.

"Soon." His brother waved a nonchalant hand toward Jordan Lake. "Cultivate something with her. It's a dirty job, but somebody's gotta do it."

Their father turned again, this time with a stern look at Adam.

The respective counsels droned on. Nick shifted impatiently. He'd felt duty-bound to stand by his father today on the first day of the trial, but there was no way he could afford to be here all day, every day for the next week or however long the trial lasted. That would fall to Adam, who'd come home for a few weeks' holiday and to support his father through the trial.

To his right, Nick caught a flash of tanned leg as Jordan shifted. His eyes lingered on her black pump-clad foot as it bounced up and down. Was she as bored and impatient as he was? Hell, she had nowhere else to be. She didn't work, unless you counted the pursuit of a good time work.

The hair on the back of his neck prickled and Nick looked up. The heiress was watching him, her mouth slanted in a cool smirk. Then she tilted her head toward her mother and whispered in her ear.

Adam cast him an amused glance, seeing the direction of his gaze. "You know you want to," he murmured.

Nick gave his brother a wry smile. It was great having him around. Nick missed him, even though their father constantly played them off against each other, unheeding of Adam's wish to have nothing to do with the family business.

Randall raised them with an abiding fascination for money, but Adam preferred to be at the cutting edge while Nick liked to have his finger on the pulse, maintaining and building strength. Adam departed four years ago to live his dream as a trader in London's stock exchange.

At the break, his father and lawyer seemed supremely confident, Randall declaring none too softly that he intended to annihilate Syrius Lake, whatever it took. With a sinking heart, Nick realized that if it wasn't this case, it would be something else. Without his mother's tempering influence, Randall would stop at nothing to get his revenge—and that directly impacted on Nick's future. He intended to be named successor of Thorne Financial Enterprises when his father retired in a few weeks. *If* his father retired…

Adam's words played over in his mind. Could he honestly consider cultivating something with Jordan Lake? Putting an end to the bitterness their fathers had supped on for three decades? The more he thought about it, the more he agreed with Adam. His eyes followed the swing of her ponytail as she walked ahead of him back into the courtroom and a smile tugged at the corners of his mouth. Jordan Lake would be the ultimate takeover.

Days later, Nick stirred as the mattress shifted and the woman next to him rose and walked into the bathroom. Sated, a little sleepy from the late nights he'd been keeping since his brother hit town, he wondered idly if he'd drifted off.

In a few short weeks, Adam would be gone, back to the high-velocity stock exchange world he ruled. Privately, Nick worried how long his brother could handle the pressure. He might be flavor of the month now, lauded by all and making an absolute fortune. But that was the thing about the share market. There was a never-ending supply of hungry young sharks circling, just waiting until someone made a mistake. Adam had been one of them not so long ago.

Nick stretched and plumped up his pillows, resting one arm behind his head. The bathroom door opened and a tall, slender blonde walked into the room. She moved to the dresser mirror, her arms raised as she fiddled with her long, tawny hair. Nick's eyes feasted on the long line of her spine, the curvaceous swell of her hips, and her skin, which had a luster to it even with the heavy drapes drawn against the afternoon sun. He liked how at ease she seemed about her nudity.

"Got time for a drink or are you rushing off?" he asked, aware that his question would surprise her. They didn't make a habit of small talk after their lovemaking sessions.

She flicked him a curious look in the mirror and continued twisting her hair expertly into a knot that looked at once messy but sophisticated.

"Let me guess." Nick clicked his tongue. "Cocktails. The Zeus Bar."

Again, he felt the wash of cool blue in her glance as she turned. "A little early for me." She bent and plucked something from the floor.

Clothing would be scattered all over, he thought. It was always like that. The moment they were inside the room, there was no decorum, no neatly undressing and folding and hanging. Sometimes they were lucky to get out of here without ripped garments.

Today she'd worn a short fuchsia shift dress, with a strap over one shoulder tied in a big extravagant bow. Easy to get in—and out—of, and entirely suitable for cocktails in any of the bars she was frequently photographed at, although never with him.

Despite her accessible outfit, it had still seemed to take an age to get his hands on her today. Time moved like a slow-motion movie clip when he entered this suite at the five-star hotel every Friday. Each image burned into his brain: the silkiness and fragrance of her creamy skin, the tumble of her hair as he tugged it into disarray, her sighs as he bared her to his hungry mouth and hands. As if she, too, had pictured this moment, his kisses and touch, the way he tore at her clothing. As if she, too, had longed for it every day between. Each set of images stayed with him, replayed over and over in his mind throughout the week until he could have her again.

Once a week for four months, and Nick knew nothing personal about her, except for what she brought to his bed.

"I saw you on TV last night," he commented as she untwisted her panties from her dress. "A short, puffy black skirt." He paused. "And a tall puffy pale man."

The woman daintily stepped into her underwear. "Not me. I stayed home last night."

Nick's mouth went dry at the little shimmy her hips did to facilitate the placement of her underwear. "I'd know those legs anywhere," he countered mildly. "I could sculpt them."

She blinked, shaking out her dress. Probably wondering what on earth did it have to do with him, he thought.

"I do have a short black puffy skirt, and—" a breathy huff of amusement burst from her lips "—a tall puffy man or two, but it wasn't last night."

She raised her arms fluidly and the dress floated down like a pink cloud, veiling her body.

Nick gazed at her, desire curling its claws into him again. Even after two tumultuous orgasms in less than two hours, he wanted her again, quite savagely. "Where do you go, Jordan Lake, when you leave my bed?"

Jordan had managed to lower her brows and close her gaping mouth by the time the dress passed over her head. She wasn't bothered that he didn't believe her about last night—she owed him no explanations. It often happened that on a slow news day, the press or TV used file pictures of her on a night out. It had been a couple of weeks since she had worn that skirt.

What surprised her was that he'd asked. They had been meeting here every Friday for four months and Nick Thorne never once expressed an interest in her activities outside of this suite.

She turned her back, arching a brow at him in the mirror. "Jealous, Nick?" she asked, deliberately imparting an edge of sarcasm.

She recalled blushing the color of this dress after their very first time together. She'd lain in bed, covers drawn up to her chin, waiting for him to return from the bathroom. What next? she'd wondered. Would they talk? Cuddle?

But Nick made it painfully obvious that this was merely a sexual arrangement. He had quickly dressed, commanded her to be here the same time next week, pressed her hand to his mouth and was out of there in five minutes flat. No backward glance, no promise to call. Nothing.

Jordan had been shocked, a little hurt and felt foolish. He thought she knew the game but she wasn't nearly as sexually experienced as the media portrayed her to be. Of her four previous lovers, two of those were fairly serious relationships. It was just that her taste in men ran to playboys, pro athletes and musicians. But her wild days were definitely behind her by the time she met Nick.

Holding his gaze, she carefully tied the bow on her shoulder and then reached behind her to tug at the zipper of her dress.

Nick threw back the covers and in a second, stood behind her, his knuckles pressing purposefully into every nub of her spine as he worked the zipper slowly up.

He took her breath away, even after all this time. His shoulders seemed an aircraft wing-span across compared to her narrow frame. He was a full head taller than her, his short, dark hair a little disheveled. In the dimly-lit room, he looked almost Latin with his thick dark brows, dusky skin and full, sensuous lips.

Lips that brushed her ear, generating a flutter of excitement deep in her belly.

Bad sign. She should definitely go. Her mother was expecting her for dinner, anyway.

But then his eyes locked on to hers in the reflection and he bent his head to nuzzle at the top of her shoulder. "No hurry, is there?"

Jordan leaned her head back to nestle in his throat, watching him with half-closed eyes. Behind her, his hand continued its slow progress, now in between her shoulder blades, each centimeter a wand of heat that caused her back to arch. She sent a silent apology to her mother for her anticipated lateness.

Nick Thorne was irresistible to her. It had been that way since the first clash of their eyes in an elevator in this very hotel. She was leaving an aunt's eightieth birthday afternoon tea party. Nick was leaving a banking conference. A chance meeting so powerful, she couldn't believe they'd even made it out of the elevator without her skin blistering. The intense attraction led to an indecently quick drink at the bar and an even more indecent mutual decision to take a room, there and then. The thrill of it all was intensified by how forbidden it was because of the hatred between their fathers for the last thirty years.

The zipper was fully up but Nick's green-gold gaze was not that of someone who wanted her dressed. He caressed the back of her neck close to her hairline, an exquisite touch that made her breath catch. The heat of him behind her, naked and masculine, bathed her skin. He slowly moved his hand to the bow on her shoulder, watching her as if challenging her to stop him. The ribbon had as much resistance as her mind, and the front panel of the dress collapsed in front but was supported by the zipper at back. Not supported enough for the weight of her breasts, which spilled out, taut and aroused.

"Now look what I've done," Nick murmured in her ear. "And I was only trying to get to know you better."

Jordan swallowed and raised her hands, cupping her breasts. "You know me," she said breathlessly, playing the game. "You know these."

"Yes, I know these." His big hands relieved hers of their burden, kneading and squeezing just the way she liked. Jordan welcomed the onslaught of sensations that had become familiar yet never failed to render her boneless. Even as she wondered vaguely why the sudden interest, it was beyond her to resist his touch. She swirled in a hazy pool of delight at his breath on her neck, his hands on her flesh, the hot, hard wall of him pressed up against her back.

He used his hands unhurriedly, feathering down her sides to her buttocks, pausing to caress them in a circular motion that made her shiver.

"I know these…" he murmured as his hands slid over the sensitive backs of her thighs, down to her knees and up again, the fabric of the dress slipping and sliding over her smooth skin, higher and higher until it was bunched around her hips.

Her breath came in shallow gasps now as he held her captive in front of him. She ought to feel wanton and ashamed, watching them in the mirror, observing her total submission to his hands, his mouth as he nibbled and licked her neck and the top of her shoulder. This was, after all, what everyone expected of her. A spoiled, rich, man-eating socialite who spent her entire life in the pursuit of pleasure.

She was on her way to perdition and pleased about it, she thought, feeling the scrape of her panties down her legs. When Nick Thorne touched her, she felt beautiful and proud that he wanted her. He was a man of substance, successful and wealthy in his own right, not some flighty playboy. Their relationship may be based on the most primitive of urges, but his desire for her, the passion he evoked from her, made her feel his equal. Love didn't come into it, but Friday afternoons were the best thing in Jordan's life and she wouldn't give them up.

She brought her fingertips down to the dresser to steady herself, just as his thigh wedged between her trembling legs, nudging them apart. His breath skittered up the length of her back, making every downy hair stand to quivering attention. Anticipation backed up in her throat.

"I know this," he insisted, his fingers lightly probing while she moaned softly, her eyes closing to contain the most sublime pleasure.

He shifted closer. A red-hot streak of sensation ripped through her and she realized it wasn't his fingers probing and gliding now, sliding in between her legs. The weight of him leaning over her back forced her forward and she pressed her palms down on the dresser, bracing herself.

"Open your eyes, Jordan," he instructed, sliding one arm around her waist.

Her head lolled heavily back and hit his chest. She pried her eyes open and found his, fierce and compelling, staring back at her through the mirror.

"Does it bother you," he asked roughly, "this secret of ours? This thing between us?"

Jordan was past reason. She wanted much more of "this thing" between them, and she wanted it now. She stared at him, pushing back into his body, squeezing her thighs together to trap him.

With an effort almost too much to bear, she forced her mouth to open, to speak. "I know the score, Nick," she told him tightly. "I'm playing the game."

Sex.

Simple. Sensational. Secret.

It was what she wanted. What she lived for. Her Friday afternoon delight.

Two

"It's all right for you," the stooped man with the trembling hands told her belligerently. "You get paid to sit around all day. I had to take the morning off work and now it looks like I won't get seen at all."

"I'm sorry, Mr. Hansen. It's been very busy this morning." Jordan tried to warm him up with a sympathetic smile but the man sighed loudly and stomped back to his seat in the crowded waiting room.

She exhaled slowly. Not even lunchtime and already a tension headache throbbed dully in her temples.

It was her turn on the voluntary roster to work two full days in Reception at the Elpis Free Clinic, and just occasionally, uncharitable though it was, she found it a little overwhelming dealing with unwell people. Thinking she was unobserved, she dropped her head down onto her arms for a second.

Behind her, Reverend Russ Parsons put his hand on her shoulder and she jerked up.

"You should have told him that no one gets paid around here. Not the doctors, cleaners, admin staff or our beautiful receptionist."

Jordan laughed ruefully. "Some receptionist! Some days I just don't seem to have the knack with people."

"You'll never get it right all of the time, but what's important is that you try so hard." He took some leaflets from the counter in front of them and handed them to her. "Why don't you give him some info on our natural healing classes?"

She took them, silently berating herself for not thinking of it.

In addition to the free clinic, the Elpis Foundation she'd set up a year ago helped Russ's parish to identify at-risk families who were stretched financially. They also provided a raft of self-help courses. Jordan was incredibly proud of the strides they'd made in a short time, but her lack of work experience spoke volumes about how she had chosen to spend her time up until recently.

"Are we still on for the Working Bee this weekend?" Russ had turned to go but stopped at the door.

Jordan nodded enthusiastically. She had recently purchased an old backpackers hostel in the beautiful Marlborough Sounds at the top of the South Island. The hostel had gone out of business years ago and was rundown and neglected, but with the volunteers from Russ's parish, she hoped to develop it into a retreat for the families in the program who never got to have a holiday. "How many are coming? I'll book the ferry tickets."

"Ten. Is Friday afternoon all right? I'll have to get the late ferry back on Saturday for services on Sunday."

Friday afternoon? Jordan's heart lurched. She shook her head and lowered her eyes, feeling the onset of an embarrassed blush. "Sorry. You guys could go but I won't be able to until Saturday morning." Philanthropy was one thing; denying herself Nick Thorne's body quite another—especially on her birthday. "My parents are putting on a thing for my birthday."

A "thing" by her father's standards would probably cost the annual wage of four or five of the people in the waiting room combined. This year, her twenty-sixth, she had prevailed upon Syrius not to go too over-the-top. "You're welcome to come," she added lamely, hoping Russ would decline. Her father didn't approve of the way she spent her time and money and she was afraid his infamous lack of tact would offend the gentle reverend.

Syrius Lake was a man of unfashionable and inflexible opinions, especially to do with women. They were to be protected and indulged but not to be taken seriously in the workforce. "I didn't work my fingers to the bone so that my princess would have to," he was fond of saying.

That made her cringe these days but Jordan had made

the most of her privileged upbringing for a long time—way too long—before coming to the realization that being a princess was a fairly boring existence.

"Speaking of invitations," Russ said as she rounded the reception counter, leaflets in hand and Mr. Hansen in her sights, "this charity ball and auction you're organizing…shouldn't we be promoting it? It's only a couple of weeks away."

Jordan paused, aware that this project departed somewhat from the more conventional fund-raising activities of the church, but the Elpis Foundation, though closely affiliated, was not a religious organization. "It's not that sort of auction, Russ. It's more of—" she searched for the right word. If there was one thing Jordan Lake knew, it was rich people and parties "—an event. It's invite only and no press."

She knew how to put on a classy yet original function, and she'd managed this one on the cheap. She would pay the orchestra herself but the ballroom was gratis, courtesy of her mother's old dancing contacts. Friends in a local venue management company had agreed to take care of the lighting and decorating for nothing. She had plenty of "volunteers" as wait staff since she'd promised an amazing after-party. The champagne hadn't been confirmed yet but the *coup-de-gras*—the catering—was coming together nicely. A truckload of fish and chips would be delivered on the night to astound the ballgown-and-tuxedo-wearing guests, courtesy of an old beau whose family owned a chain of fast-food restaurant outlets. Jordan was notorious enough to be able to pull off such a cheeky gesture. "It's all in hand," she assured Russ. "At this stage we have about a hundred people coming, but I have a bit more time."

Russ pursed his lips. "I'm sure if we advertise, we can do better than that."

"Russ, that's a hundred extremely wealthy people, the movers and shakers of the country. Trust me, the really rich want discretion with their philanthropy."

He smiled wryly. "Is that why you're so reluctant to put your name on all the good work you do?"

Jordan shot him a warning look. "No one takes me seriously. The kind of publicity people associate with me is not the kind of publicity I want for the Elpis Foundation. That was the condition of me setting it up. It's better that way, believe me."

Famous for being famous… She walked into the waiting room, determined to make Mr. Hansen like her. Forever the focus of the newspapers and TV cameras but for all the wrong reasons, even though she had toned it down over the last year. Reporters didn't care a jot if most of what they wrote was wrong. Philanthropy was a serious business and she needed to protect the Elpis Foundation. It was her one redeeming feature.

On Friday morning, Jordan passed Nick in the corridor of the High Court. He paused as they drew level, looking straight ahead. Since court was in session, there were few people around.

"See you at three?" he asked in a low voice.

Her pulse skittered as it always did when she looked at him. His presence in the courtroom for most of this week had underlined her desire for him and the forbidden thrill she got from knowing that he wanted her.

But they had to take care. It wasn't just the stress her father was under. Nick was different. Somehow, she wanted to keep him to herself.

She hadn't expected the amount of public interest there was in the case—every day she ran the gauntlet of photographers and reporters, all of whom seemed more interested in what she was wearing and how her love life was than the actual semantics of the trial.

"Nick, there are so many reporters," she whispered back. "Don't you think we should cool it, just till this trial is over?"

He turned his head and met her eyes and Jordan's heartbeat went wild. If eyes were the windows to hell, then Nick was on fire—for her. Right now, this moment.

Her knees turned to water.

Nick nudged her toward the stairwell a few steps away. She kept her head down, aware that if anyone looked at her face, they'd know exactly what she was thinking—that she wanted his hands, his mouth on her. Preferably both and *now* would be good.

He pushed through the door, her hot on his heels, then turned and crowded her against the wall, his arms resting on the wall above her head. The rest of his body did not touch her at all.

The sweep of his eyes over her face, down her body

and back again, was a tangible caress. Thankful for the support of the wall at her back, Jordan pressed into it, squirming with a restless heat.

His face was close—not close enough, but close.

"You want to 'cool it?'" Nick demanded in a hot whisper.

"I don't *want* to," she whispered back. "Your reputation as a steady, conservative banker will suffer a lot more than mine if we're caught."

"It's driving me mad, seeing you in there," he growled. "So close, not able to touch."

She reeled with the need to touch him, and with her own panic. Nick had never done anything so reckless before. "Oh, Nick, this is dangerous."

"I haven't touched you," he murmured, his eyes burning. "Yet."

He knew, as Jordan did, that if he touched her, she'd offer no resistance, despite the fear of discovery.

"Someone is going to walk through that door any minute," she cautioned him.

His eyes tracked a heated path, lingering on her lips, then in slow, hot increments down her body. "All part of the fun, isn't it?"

Their eyes met. Clearly, steady and conservative Nick Thorne was as hooked on the danger of the situation as she was.

She shifted again, craving his touch, knowing she shouldn't. It was torture being this close, seeing him this excited, yet denying her.

His hand landed in her hair, then moved around to

cup her chin. Despite her alarm, her lips parted in anticipation.

Nick stared down, his thumb moving softly over her cheek. "You are seriously beautiful."

Her eyes flew wide. That was new, too. Nick preferred a more earthy flavor to his compliments, more show, don't tell. The daily exposure in the courtroom must be having an effect on him as well.

Meantime, his gaze moved down to her mouth, stayed, heated. His thumb circled down and laid on her bottom lip. His face bent, inched closer. He was, quite simply, driving her mad. Who cared if anyone saw? She clamped her lips around his thumb, drawing it slowly into her mouth. Nick's eyes widened, and then some more when she swirled her tongue around the tip. Two could play at that, she thought triumphantly, watching the torture darken his eyes.

But then he slid his thumb slowly out of her mouth. "Cool it? I don't think so. I'll see you at three o clock."

He stepped back and Jordan ducked smartly out from under him. She looked back as she passed through the heavy door. He still leaned on the wall, his head raised, looking after her.

The cooler air of the corridor was a welcome relief. Away from Nick's potent presence, she pressed her hand on her stomach, aflutter with nerves. Even if he was willing to take the risk, she couldn't embarrass her father while he was under so much stress.

Still, her mind and body hummed with anticipation. Instinctively, she knew that their afternoon rendezvous would have more bite to it than usual.

* * *

Spending every morning in court was impacting his work, so Nick sighed when the intercom buzzed and his personal assistant's voice informed him that his brother was here. The door opened and Adam appeared, looking relaxed in jeans and a leather jacket. He turned side-on to Nick's desk and approximated a smooth golf swing. "It's a beautiful day, big brother. What say you play hooky for the afternoon and we hit the golf course for a quick nine?"

Nick shook his head. In little under an hour, he would be at the hotel, relieving a certain heiress of her clothes. And for that reward, he didn't care if he had to work all weekend to catch up. "I have an appointment."

Adam frowned and flopped down in a chair facing Nick. "Cancel it."

"If I get this backlog cleared tonight, I might be free tomorrow," Nick said with a pointed look at the stack of papers in front of him.

Jasmine, his personal assistant, appeared at the door. "Would you like coffee?"

Adam spun around in his chair. "I would, thank you, Jas*mina*."

The beautiful brunette blushed and turned away.

Nick frowned. Adam had a hide like a rhino. No way could he have missed Nick's "I'm busy" hint. And the last thing he needed was his Casanova brother upsetting his workplace. "Stop flirting with my personal assistant."

Adam turned back to him. "Why? Something going on with you two?"

"Adam, she works for me."

"So? If she worked for me, I'd add to her job description."

Nick sighed and made a show of checking his watch.

"I thought you should know," Adam began, "Dad's been ear-bashing me over lunch again about staying on and giving you a hand."

The real reason for his visit… "I don't need a hand," Nick said in a long-suffering tone.

"I know that, Nick. You have more than earned your place at the helm of this ship. I have no intention of muscling in on your territory."

Nick's jaw tightened. "There's the rub. It isn't my territory, is it?"

It was Randall Thorne's greatest wish that both sons run his empire after he retired. No matter how often Adam resisted, his father never stopped trying to lure him back from London. The disbursement of their mother's will last year had shocked the brothers and delighted their father. Instead of a sizeable chunk of the company shares going to Nick, as everyone expected, he got baubles and a beach house and Adam got the shares. Whether his mother intended it or not, she had handed his father a lofty weapon to pit brother against brother. To delay, yet again, announcing his retirement and naming Nick as his successor.

"Dad was nearly resigned to the fact that you didn't want it," Nick said moodily. "But now—he'll do anything to have both of us on board."

"The will stated that I can't sell my shares to you, but

I can vote with you, Nick. Tell me how you want to play it. And remember, the old man can't put off retiring forever—he's seventy next month."

"Since Mom died, there is no reining him in." Nick scowled at the newspaper on his desk. "Her past friendship with Elanor Lake was the only thing that stopped him from going after Syrius years ago. He's using the court case as another tactic to postpone announcing his retirement." He reached out and turned the paper toward Adam. A good portion of the front page covered the court case—and Jordan Lake's wardrobe. "If it's not one thing, it's another." His mother's illness and subsequent death, Adam's presence or absence—his father threw excuse after excuse into the pot to put off the inevitable.

Adam nodded thoughtfully. "I'm pretty sure he's got something else up his sleeve to get at Syrius. He was being very cagey at lunch, always a sign that he's plotting something."

Nick tugged on his earlobe, a wry grin on his face. "I've tried telling him that once he's retired, he can spend twenty-three hours a day going after Syrius Lake if he wants to, but he's adamant he wants to bury him before he retires."

Nick wasn't alone in thinking his father would win the defamation case, but had a nasty feeling that the small victory wouldn't appease him for long.

Adam cast an interested eye over the newspaper. There was a footnote to the court case: Jordan Lake's birthday bash tonight, organized by her father. The paper called it an "ostentatious display of wealth." He tapped the paper idly. "I told you. The best way to stop this stupid feud is to get Jordan Lake to fall for you. That man cannot, it seems, deny his little girl anything."

Before Nick could respond, Jasmine entered with a tray. She set it down on Nick's desk and lifted the coffeepot. Adam leaned in closer than he had to, Nick noticed, and held up a cup, smiling into her face. "How long have you worked for my brother, Jasmine? Must be nearly five years."

Jasmine blushed to the roots of her severely pulled back auburn hair. "Yes, I—ah—think so. Nick?" She raised her eyes to him.

Nick nodded, mildly surprised by her discomfort. He'd known English-born Jasmine for years. Her composure was legendary. "Have I told you, Jasmine, that my younger brother is nothing but a flirt and not to be taken seriously?"

He noticed the slight tremble in her hand as she poured the coffee, and how resolutely she kept her eyes on the task at hand and nowhere near Adam's face. Could his calm, efficient, very proper personal assistant have a thing for Adam?

Adam raised the full cup and saluted her. "Why don't you give all this up and come work for me? London's where it's at."

Jasmine kept her eyes averted and poured Nick's coffee, apologizing when she slopped a little in the saucer.

"Thanks," Nick said drily as she finished and left the room.

He glanced at his brother and warned, "Don't even think about it. She is much too good for you."

Adam turned his palms up innocently, then glanced toward the door. "You work too hard if you haven't noticed how very lovely she is, in a quiet sort of way."

"I don't want you messing with her," Nick told him shortly. "Good staff are hard to find, and you're leaving soon." His brother's trail of broken hearts stretched a million miles.

Adam shook his head, amused. "You're too good, Nicky. You wouldn't dream of tupping your personal assistant, just as you wouldn't dream of going after Jordan Lake and risking Dad's wrath. Mom was right, you need to live a little."

That was a low and quite unnecessary dig. His brother referred to the letter Melanie Thorne had left with her lawyer to give to Nick at the will reading. "You're a good son, Nick, strong, ambitious and loyal." Christ, he sounded like a golden retriever! "But it's time you learned to live. Want something you shouldn't. Take something you have no right to. Fight the good fight and have some fun."

He didn't know what the hell his mother was on about, but she was right in that he always did the expected thing.

After Adam had gone, Nick got up and opened his office safe. Inside were three jewelry boxes, his bequest from his mother, gifts from his father over the years. There was a blue diamond cluster ring, a necklace with a centerpiece of a four carat blue diamond and a pair of blue diamond earrings.

Nick had the relevant documents from the IGI, the

world's largest gem certification and appraisal institute. He knew the worth of the stones. He also knew that his mother would expect him to present these priceless gifts to his bride one day. And Nick always did what was expected of him, didn't he?

He glanced at the newspaper on his desk. She wouldn't expect him to give blue diamonds to Jordan Lake, he was sure of that. Neither would his brother, and his father would probably disown him if he found out.

Nick closed the ring box and returned it to the safe, wondering what Jordan herself would think if her Friday lover gave her diamonds. He lost himself for a long moment, imagining the incredulity in her blue eyes.

He closed the necklace box, berating himself for even considering changing the dynamic of a relationship—a good relationship—based on sex.

His hand reached toward the box containing the earrings, and at that point, he fully intended closing it and replacing it in the safe with the others. But something made him pause and lift the box toward the light above. Would she wear them? She might if she recognized that the jewel's electric blue were very similar to her own eyes, especially when she was helpless with lust—like earlier in the stairwell.

He closed the box and put it in his pocket. Nick was going to do something irresponsible for once. Not for her or for anyone else. Just for himself.

Three

Later that day, as the first mad rush of desire ebbed away, Nick rolled out of bed and picked up his suit jacket from the floor. "I have something for you."

Jordan lay in the middle of the big bed with the sheet pulled up around her middle, a sharp contrast between the pristine white sheet and her lightly-tanned body. The slight flush on her skin was fading, her breathing more steady than a minute ago. She lifted her chin, watching him curiously.

"But first…" Nick grabbed the edge of the sheet and tugged it away, leaving her naked.

She maneuvered herself into a sitting position and crossed her long legs at the ankles, but made no effort to clutch at the sheet or cover herself. He liked that she was totally without guile or vanity in this room. It occurred to him that he also felt comfortable standing, walking around in front of her naked. Had he ever felt this level of ease with a casual girlfriend before?

Unable to recall, he offered her the jewelry box.

Jordan hesitated before taking it, her eyes on his face. "A birthday gift?" Her voice was low and puzzled.

Nick perched on the edge of the bed. "If you like."

She dragged her eyes off his face and opened the box. Her mouth moved in surprise, a soundless question. She tilted the box this way and that and finally spoke, still looking at the earrings. "Nick, a man gives me diamonds. What am I supposed to think about that?"

He shrugged. "Don't think about it at all."

She looked up at him, a crease of perplexity between her eyes that he'd never seen before. He silently cursed himself for confusing her. What was he thinking, messing with the natural order of things? "Don't read anything into it," he said a little roughly. "I believe I thought more of my own pleasure than yours."

The little frown deepened, as if she couldn't make sense of it.

Damn Adam and his crazy notions. Nick exhaled loudly and leaned toward her. He picked up one of the precious, glinting jewels, brushed her hair behind her ears and went about fitting it. "They matched your eyes. I wanted to see you naked, wearing only these. That's it."

That wasn't it. Hadn't he done it because he was sick of being labeled the good son, the one who never rocked the boat?

Her face cleared, as if she'd solved a riddle. "They're a gift for your mistress."

Nick's lip curled in distaste. He hated that word. "I don't think of you as my mistress. Neither of us is married. We're free to indulge ourselves."

She gazed at him solemnly. Nick picked up the other earring, pried the butterfly clip off and indicated that she turn her head.

She obeyed. "What *do* you think of me as then?"

"If we have to put a label on it, I'd call you my luxury," he said as he pushed the other earring through the piercing in her lobe. He secured the post and drew back, looking at her face.

"Your luxury." She nodded and her smile was without reproach. "I'll save them just for this room. They'll be our secret."

Nick sat back, admiring his handiwork, thinking she did indeed look spellbindingly luxurious. Her golden hair, a mass of loose curls today, cascaded over her shoulders like the caps of a choppy sea captured and molded in gold. Yesterday, in court she'd worn it straight and smooth.

And then her words hit him, or more, her tone. Had he imagined a slightly sarcastic edge to her voice?

Nick dropped his hands to his bare knees. "I'm not ashamed." Not of her. Maybe of himself for confusing her. "Hell, Jordan! They're yours. Do what you want with them. Sell them, if it pleases you."

Hurt showed in the little press of her lips and the way she suddenly looked away from him. "I don't need any *more* money from a Thorne," she said quietly.

Nick had made a real pig's ear of this. An off-the-cuff gesture and he'd ended up bringing the past into this room. He should have remembered that whatever this madness was between them, the past would always be a barrier.

Thirty years ago, Nick's father was driving the two couples home from a night out when a tragic accident nearly claimed the life of Syrius Lake's pregnant wife. The injuries she had suffered put her in a wheelchair for life and killed her unborn son, but five years later she endured a difficult pregnancy and gave birth to Jordan. Lake never forgave Randall Thorne and when his financial situation worsened because of high medical costs, he demanded assistance. Randall signed over a huge valuable block of real estate in Wellington's CBD, with the understanding that when Syrius was able, he would repay the loan. But on the day of Jordan's birth, the bitter ex-friend transferred the property to his daughter's name.

Prevailed upon by guilt and his own wife, Randall Thorne let it ride, but it rankled. Both men went on to become business icons in New Zealand's capital city and the bad blood simmered away, helped along by repeated sniping from both camps.

So technically, Jordan was rich on Thorne money, but Nick didn't care about that. It wasn't her fault or his. It just was.

He put his index finger under her chin and turned her face to look at him. "I'm sorry. I didn't intend to hurt you…"

Her smile, when it came, was more rueful than hurt.

"You haven't." She lifted her hands and touched her new adornments. "I'll wear them with pride."

Nick's instincts were right on the nail about how perfectly the blue diamonds matched her eye color. They gazed at each other, gratitude and regret gradually giving way to an acute awareness of where they were, what they were to each other. The urgency escalated, the air between them smoldered with its hot breath.

They moved toward each other in a rush, their hands reaching greedily. She was fine, they were fine, nothing had changed. He'd done the right thing, giving her blue diamonds that twinkled and trembled with desire and anticipation when he pushed her down on the bed, ravaging her mouth. That warmed with sultry promise as he drew her arms up over her head and moved into position. That exploded with blue sparks when he filled her, an inexorable upward motion into infinite pleasure…and crackled with the fury of reaching for, overtaking, plunging into blissful release.

He'd done the right thing giving her the earrings and who cared if was for her or for him? They'd both enjoy them.

But somehow, he left the hotel feeling he'd missed an opportunity of some kind, or they both had. If Jordan Lake was his luxury, could he pay the price?

Jordan was late for her own birthday party. She rushed up the stairs of the up-market club, apologizing loudly, knowing her parents expected her half an hour ago.

She needn't have worried. Everything was under

control and most of the guests hadn't arrived yet. The champagne was chilled and delicious, the lighting perfect, security on the door. Of the expected one hundred and fifty guests, twenty or so would be friends of hers, the rest would be her parents' friends, business colleagues, local celebrities in the arts, politics and sports and a smattering of reporters and photographers. Jordan would pose with all the usual suspects, regulars of the It crowd. And then she would go home alone, as she had for most of the last year. Even her father would yawn at her lifestyle these days—except for her Friday afternoons.

She bent to kiss her mother, knowing this was the last real kiss she'd get all night. As she drew back, her mother's hands firmed on her cheeks for a few seconds, holding her. Elanor Lake frowned at the earrings. "They're lovely, darling. Where did you get them?"

She hadn't been able to resist wearing them no matter how often she told herself to lock them away. But, oh, they were so beautiful, and Nick hadn't said not to wear them. He hadn't even stipulated that she wasn't to tell who gave them to her.

Vanity won. The earrings were perfect with the pale yellow dress she wore, lending it a hint of boldness.

Jordan straightened and flicked her hand in the air. "Just one of my many admirers."

Her mother gave her a measured look. "Which admirer is giving you blue diamonds?"

Her father snorted. "Anything less than diamonds, then he isn't worth his salt, princess," he declared.

One by one, the beautiful people arrived and she laughed and kissed air so many times, her lips were bruised. But often, she touched the earrings and her thoughts turned to the confusing man who'd given them to her.

The extravagant gift had blown her away. Up to now, Nick was the only man she'd met who'd been completely straight about what he wanted from her—her body. There were no expectations past that, on either side. Their weekly meetings in the luxury Presidential Suite were all about an extraordinary attraction and nothing else.

She couldn't put her finger on when things had started to feel different, but it was recent. He'd changed. Suddenly he was asking questions, taking risks, talking to her. He'd watched her today as if trying to divine her thoughts. Hurt her a little by admitting he'd thought more of his own pleasure in giving her the gift. Then again, that admission spoke volumes for a man who was so spare with words: he saw something beautiful; he thought of her.

But it hurt her more when he reminded her of the origins of her trust fund, and the reason they could never have more than they had right now.

Her oldest friend, Julie, dragged her onto the dance floor and she happily acquiesced. But her mind strayed often to Nick. Jordan looked around at the glitzy lights and gay smiles, wondering if he'd like this sort of place? Would her friends like him, and vice versa? Was he a dancer? When it came down to it, she knew so little about him, just that they fit together perfectly in the bedroom.

"Oh, my God! Look-it!" Julie pointed through the throng to a tall, handsome man leaning on the bar, looking their way. "Isn't that…?"

Jordan looked over and her heart did a weird slide. "John West," she said in dismay.

Jordan's first heartbreak. She'd been in her first year at high school, he in his last. His interest in her caused a ripple of excitement through all her friends; someone of his stature expressing interest in a first year was unheard of.

Alas, the romance floundered quickly.

"Let's see if we can pick who he's here with," her friend said.

Jordan wondered if it was the same girlfriend he'd dumped her for two days after he'd first crooked his brow at her, commanding her to parade around the school quadrant with him like his queen.

She shrugged and turned away. Although it was a minor blip on her heartstrings that she hadn't thought of in years, the one thing that stuck was the crushing real-ization that despite her money and social standing, she wasn't smart enough, pretty enough, interesting enough to hold his attention, not even for a week! Her father's shameless indulgence reminded her that the world saw her as a bubble-headed trophy with only her wealth to offer. She knew better. She was different now, more than that.

Nick Thorne was the real deal—respected, smart, ambitious and successful. Whatever he called it, she was his mistress. She'd live up to his expectations in that regard, but she'd do her best to protect her heart.

* * *

On Monday, the court clerk announced the lunch break to sighs of relief. The morning had dragged. Nick looked forward to getting back to his office, if only for a break from the steel thread of sexual tension that came with sitting ten feet away from the object of his desire, and the knowledge that it would be four torturous days before he could have her again.

Suddenly the wiry figure of Syrius Lake bounded across the aisle. His face was an interesting shade of plum. He sidestepped Randall's counsel and stood defiantly in front of the complainant's bench.

"Randall Thorne," he rumbled, his deep voice belying his rather slight frame. "Keep your pup away from my daughter."

Nick's heart stopped and he involuntarily flicked a glance at Jordan. She had jumped to her feet, and stood with one leg in front of the other, ready for flight, the line of her body taut with tension. Her eyes were huge but they were on her father, not him.

Randall rose, towering over Syrius, the table in between them. Nick rose, too, and brushed past Adam to stand by his father's side.

"Nick's got too much sense…" Randall began.

"Not him." Syrius pointed a long, bony finger at Adam, still seated in the row behind.

Adam! Nick turned his head slowly, and in those few seconds, everything inside him went cold, and his throat closed as if gripped by a vise.

His brother raised his brows in studied nonchalance

and shrugged. "I hooked up with a couple of lovelies at a bar, tagged along to a party. How was I supposed to know it was Jordan's birthday bash?"

Through the ice-cold rage bathing his belly, Nick barely noted that Adam directed his explanation—and a quizzical look—at him, rather than Syrius.

All around people had stopped, enthralled by the drama. And then his father gave the crowd what they wanted.

"If he's a pup," he suggested, "perhaps she's a bitch in heat."

Nick tore his eyes off his brother's and glanced at Jordan's white, shocked face. He gripped his father's arm firmly. "You'll apologize for that."

"The hell I will!" Randall blustered.

The two Lake women reached Syrius. Elanor spoke in urgent whispers while Jordan grasped the sleeve of her father's suit, tugging at it ineffectually.

Randall lifted his arm in a half hearted attempt to remove it from Nick's grip.

Nick only gripped harder. "*Now*, Dad."

Accepting defeat, Randall launched a scathing glance at his enemy, cleared his throat and nodded vaguely in Jordan's direction. "I beg your pardon, Jordan." Turning back to Syrius, he raised his chin, "When I've finished mopping the floor with you here, Lake, I'm going to start all over again. I wouldn't let your lawyer take a holiday anytime soon if I were you."

"Bring it on, Thorne," Syrius snarled. He shot one last look of loathing that encompassed all three Thornes, then he stomped off with his counsel in tow, making no effort to assist Jordan with her mother's wheelchair.

Mortified, Nick couldn't look at Jordan, but as she pushed her mother's chair past him, Elanor met his eyes and gave him a distant but not unfriendly nod. Despite the ridiculous circumstances, Nick found himself admiring her for her fortitude and grace when she had more reason to hate his family than anyone. He watched until they disappeared out of the courtroom, then turned back to find his father glaring down at Adam.

"Well? What have you got to say for yourself?"

Nick's jealousy returned full force, crushing his chest and throat again. The thought of his playboy brother anywhere near Jordan incensed him. "Did you—" *touch, dance, kiss* "—speak to her at the party?" He could barely get the words past his clenched teeth.

Adam's glance was sharp as a tack. "Nick, I didn't get a toe in the door before Syrius was bleating at security to have me removed. Why?"

Intense relief laced Nick's exhalation. He unclenched his palms and they were damp. Ignoring Adam's question, he turned abruptly and reached for his jacket. The act of putting it on, gathering up his phone and brief-case, gave him a few seconds to think about that relief. *Okay, we've ascertained that I'm not fond of the thought of anyone else's hands on her. Fine. We can work this out.*

Now composed, he gave his father a stern look. "I have to get back to the office, but try and behave yourself this afternoon." He frowned at Randall. "Insult Syrius all you like, but leave his family out of it."

He strode away, allowing himself a small smile when he heard his father say to Adam, "Why can't you be more like your brother?"

Four

Nick pressed the doorbell, glowering at the peephole when he heard her ask who it was. "It's Nick. Open up, Jordan."

He still waited half a minute, tapping his thigh impatiently, until she opened the door. She peeked around the corner of the door, one hand covering her lower face. Her hesitation became immediately clear; a pale green chalky substance covered most of her face. Her hair was loose but held back from her face by a headband. She wore silky light blue pajamas, a less than welcoming expression, and her feet were bare.

That didn't mean she was off the hook. "Are you ill?"

"No." Frowning, she looked over his shoulder into

the empty corridor of her apartment building and then stepped back.

"Expecting someone?" he asked, giving her a thorough inspection.

"Do I look like I'm expecting someone?" She lifted her hand from her face and gestured him forward impatiently. "Come in before someone sees you."

Nick stepped inside and then turned and waited while she closed the door.

Jordan leaned her back against the door her skin flushing pink beneath the green facial mask. "How did you get up here?"

He shrugged. "Someone was coming up, I followed."

"Nick, you shouldn't be here."

His temper bridled. He'd been on a slow burn for about twenty-four hours now. He'd had a huge row with his father last night after confirming his plans to hire a P.I. to investigate one of Syrius's directors for corruption. It became more and more obvious that the old man had no intention of retiring any time soon, not while Syrius Lake was around to take potshots at.

Reading the papers today had turned the heat up. Nick's frustration had about hit boiling. "We had an arrangement."

"I sent you a text."

Nick swore under his breath. A text that said nothing. *Sorry, something's come up.*

He would have accepted her canceling their regular appointment if she hadn't been photographed eating a late Friday afternoon lunch with Jason Cook, the most worthless playboy on the planet. An ex-pro rugby player who destroyed hotel rooms, threw things at bartenders and went through money like water. And who'd reportedly had a steamy romance with Jordan a year ago.

His father's next potential campaign against Syrius made Nick's decision to ally himself with her all the more attractive, but the lady herself seemed comfortable with the status quo. Somehow he had to persuade her that she wanted more, knock her off balance enough to start thinking of him in a different light.

Hence the unannounced visit. It didn't hurt that the thought of Cook's hands on her infuriated him. He reached out, hooking his finger into the V of her pajama top, and pulled her into him. "You and Jason in the newspaper this morning... You want him, Jordan?"

As her unresisting body bumped against his, the impact caused the top button to slip through the hole. The material gaped as she inhaled in surprise. The creamy swell of a luscious, unfettered breast taunted him.

How many men did she share her body with? The question had tormented him for hours. How many men savored that perfect mouth, nuzzled her impossibly soft and fragrant skin.

Under his glare, her eyes sparked with annoyance and her pink cheeks burned through the green streaks. She laid her hands flat against his chest and braced against him. "I didn't realize that giving me a gift branded me as your exclusive property."

"It doesn't, but your Friday afternoons are mine, not bloody Jason Cook's."

"Jason is only a friend these days. Not—" she lifted her chin defiantly "—that it's any of your business."

"Some friend. I thought you were satisfied with our arrangement."

"I was." Her eyes flickered away and back. "I am. But I think we're being watched."

Nick raised his brows, waiting.

Sighing, she clasped the edges of her pajama top closed and pushed past him, padding down the short hallway through a stylish kitchen and to a side table in the lounge. Nick followed, his eyes closely monitoring the sensual slide of blue silk-clad hips.

Jordan picked up an envelope from the table and turned to him. "These came yesterday."

Nick took the envelope and pulled out two enlarged photographs of Jordan entering and leaving their Friday hotel, wearing a little black dress with a wide belt. He remembered it because the belt had an unusual clasp and his eager fingers had wasted at least three seconds fumbling with the damn thing. The photo was dated last Friday, their last meeting. "You're always being watched and photographed." He handed the photos back. "What of it?"

"These were couriered to me here, yesterday morning. No note. No sender details."

Nick pursed his lips. "And that was enough to send you rushing into Jason Cook's arms."

She gazed at him steadily. "Why do you suppose we went to the Backbencher's Bar, Nick?"

"Probably the only place in town he hasn't been thrown out of."

"Because it's the press's watering hole, where most of them spend their Friday afternoons. I did it to throw whoever might be watching us off the scent."

Nick processed her tone and earnest expression and battled down the jealousy bubbling in his blood. Considering the publicity surrounding the court case, she would have known her presence at that bar, especially with a man of Jason Cook's reputation, would end up in the next day's papers.

Not to make him jealous. Not to patch things up with a past lover. The relief surprised Nick with its intensity. He had to remember his purpose here tonight—keep her guessing, spike her interest. His very real jealousy was an added bonus.

Jordan shifted under his gaze as if uncomfortably aware that her face was covered in green goop. "Get yourself a drink," she told him, pointing at the small bar in the corner of the room. "I'll go and clean up."

Nick's eyes stayed with her until she turned into the first door down the hall. Her bedroom, he presumed, relieved to be left alone momentarily. It gave him a chance to explore, try to get a handle on her.

He moved fully into the lounge, his eyes busy.

Her apartment was modern, minimalist, but surprisingly homely and welcoming. One of the two black leather sofas was scattered with papers. There were more papers on the coffee table and a mug of something in the middle with steam coming off it. The expansive drapes were drawn but he'd bet there was an amazing view of the city and harbor beyond from her thirteenth story apartment. The walls were bare except in the dining nook where two large, striking sketches faced each other above her elegant dining table. One depicted a 1920s couple sitting at a table, the woman looking coyly away as the man held her arm by the wrist and above the elbow, kissing his way up her arm. The other was a couple dancing, maybe the tango, he decided.

The bar had everything he could want but Nick wasn't in the mood for alcohol. He walked to the sofa, sweeping the papers into a pile and setting them on the coffee table.

There was a property listing on top, torn from a real estate magazine. It depicted an old villa in the Marlborough Sounds at the top of the South Island. Not the sort of place Jordan would be interested in, surely. The lady could afford to buy the entire South Island. She was luxury all the way. What use would she have for a broken-down old villa?

Then again, what did he know of her likes and dislikes outside of the bedroom?

While waiting for her return, he glanced at the next item on the pile and saw a newsletter headed The Elpis Foundation. He only took note because the author was Reverend Russ Parsons, an old family friend.

Before he could read the contents, Jordan returned, her face clean and her hair released from the headband. Nick nearly smiled when he saw she'd changed. A cream sweater and soft black pants were probably safer than the lovely but flimsy pajamas. She obviously didn't trust him to keep his hands to himself.

Jordan perched on the arm of the couch, her hands restless. Her feet were still bare, toenails pearly-pink and gleaming. Nick swallowed the remnants of his unwarranted anger and jealousy, thinking that this was how she looked alone in the evenings. Freshly bathed, by the clean scent of her. Her hair brushed out and gleaming. Skin scrubbed and glowing.

She fidgeted under his scrutiny, her mouth a little sullen.

"Nice apartment," he commented pleasantly.

She glanced at his empty hands. "Did you not want a drink?"

He wasn't bothered but then again, he liked the idea of her waiting on him. It would also serve to prolong his visit, break the ice, open the way for him to try out a little charm.

"A Scotch would be good."

She hadn't expected him to say yes, he knew by the little twist of her mouth. He settled back while she prepared his drink with a kind of polite displeasure. No smile when she handed it to him, either.

Nick reached for the mug on the coffee table. The liquid inside was cooling by the pinched look of the surface. He handed it to her, thinking how improbable this was. Jordan Lake home alone on a Saturday night with only a face mask and mug of chocolate for company.

She took the mug. An awkward silence descended.

"Looking to invest in some property?" he asked, picking up the leaflet. It would be a good investment. Marlborough Sounds boasted some of the most desirable real estate in the country.

"I already bought it."

Nick looked up in surprise. "Can't see you in the DIY store, somehow."

Her mouth twitched but the smile didn't reach her eyes. "You'd be surprised."

He leaned back, spreading his arm along the back of the couch. Their eyes met and held for long seconds and that old familiar awareness arced between them. She was so naturally beautiful, larger than life beautiful, even with little or no makeup on. Nick's chest swelled when her eyes widened and then hazed over with her own recognition of the incredible desire between them. She felt it, too, he exulted, this pull that gripped his throat and stole his breath. Every time was like their first meeting in a sterile elevator. An unquenchable desire that hit him like a bullet between the eyes.

Just like now.

Jordan broke the spell and looked down into her drink. "You're—different," she said. "What's changed?"

She shifted one foot to rest on top of the other, her restlessness showing insecurities he didn't know she had.

Nick faced her fully. "I want you, Jordan," he answered truthfully. "That hasn't changed."

She looked up under her lashes. "And you can have me. On Fridays. At the hotel."

It didn't surprise him that she'd picked up on his recent change of behavior toward her. In their brief conversations to date, she'd shown a perceptive intuitiveness, eroding his assumptions that she was nothing more than a spoiled heiress who liked making an exhibition of herself.

Damn his brother for putting the thought in his head. Damn his mother for the will and her belief that he was the perennial dutiful son, and his father, too, for being such a vindictive, intransigent bastard. But for their interference, Nick would be perfectly happy with the prior arrangement. The thrill of a forbidden pleasure. A once-weekly event that, while momentous at the time, belonged in a compartment of his brain that had no bearing on how he lived his life or the decisions he made.

"Perhaps it's seeing you in court every day," he suggested. It was as good a lie as any, he supposed.

She nodded. Her feet were still playing with each other, he noticed. "By the way, I'm sorry about my father's behavior the other day."

Jordan shrugged, drawing his attention to her front, his interest quickening when he saw she wasn't wearing a bra under the soft wool.

"They're as bad as each other," she responded.

"What would Syrius do if he found out about us?" Nick probed.

She rolled her eyes. "I don't even want to think about it."

Nick knew that was his major stumbling block. He had to get her so interested, so wound up in him that she'd forget about her father's wrath.

"And yours?" she inquired politely.

He sipped his drink, wondering how truthful to be. Lies had a way of tripping you up, so it was best to keep things simple. "He wouldn't like it," he said slowly, "but it's not up to him, is it?"

Jordan sighed and looked away. "Maybe we should…"

Nick's whole being jolted in rebellion. He knew what she was going to say. Stop? No way! He was already on edge after only a week's abstinence. It was torture sitting in that courtroom day after day, watching her every move out of the corner of his eyes. Her mile-long legs crossing and uncrossing, the drift of her expensive scent, an occasional hot-blooded glance in his direction. Nick was at the end of his tether. He shook his head adamantly. "I'm not ready to give it up just yet."

Jordan pursed her lips. "And the photos?"

Nick had had enough. The desire he felt for her was too close to the surface. Besides, it wouldn't hurt to allow her to see that she affected him. Intensity so often created the same interest in the recipient.

He stood abruptly, looming over her. She raised her head just as his hands dived her hair, lifting her face to his. "You think I want this? Need this?"

Her eyes were wide with surprise. She gasped in a quick breath.

"You're like a drug to me," he gritted, glowering down. "An addiction. Every Friday, I leave that hotel and think, yes. This time, I've got her out of my system. This time…"

Despite this being about knocking her off-kilter, his own body was primed like a detonator. He exhaled, fighting for control, searching for the innate good manners and responsible behavior that had shaped his life. He was a businessman, dammit, not one of her playboys.

He gentled his hands, stroking her hair. Soothed by the silky soft strands running through his fingers. "But then I change my mind, start thinking about next Friday."

He caressed her cheek and her eyelids fluttered as he knew they would.

"It's just sex, Nick," she whispered, turning her face to press a kiss in his palm, that one small act softening her cavalier words.

In her hurry to wash, she'd missed a tiny patch of green by her earlobe and he rubbed his finger over it, his own excitement rocketing when her lips parted involuntarily on a sigh.

"Yes it is," he murmured. He stroked one finger down her throat, felt her pulse leap. She ghosted a fraction closer while keeping her backside in contact with the arm of the sofa. Her head fell back even more in invitation and he bent to nuzzle the fragrant skin under her earlobe. Soft and smooth, her skin was still slightly damp from being freshly washed. Whatever she'd used in her face mask smelled good enough to eat, to taste, again and again.

She strained up, her face turned to his. Darned if he could remember what they were talking about when her mouth bumped against his cheek. It was too much of a temptation, even though he was pretty sure he'd started the body contact not intending to kiss her, only to tease a little. To make the point that she wanted him as much as he wanted her.

Just before his lips met hers, he touched his index finger to the corner of her mouth and frowned down into eyes that smoldered with electric blue desire. "I won't give it up just yet."

Her expression softened. Dipping his head, he took her mouth, filled her mouth, sank in welcome relief. His desire flowed from him into her and back again in a heady rush. She moaned low in her throat, trying to rise, pressing up into him. Happy to help, he slid one arm down her back and brought her hard up against him. The kiss deepened, she opened for him, hungry, appealing for more, her tongue eagerly seeking his.

With one arm supporting her back, he slid the other hand under the sweater, needing the silky slide of her skin. Always when he touched her, some part of his mind registered the softness of her skin. Never had he felt such soft skin; his fingers rejoiced in it. He palmed her torso; she felt hot, so hot. She swayed, her hands clutching at the backs of his arms. Nick slid his hand up, climbing the taut slope of her breast. He heard her breath catch, felt his, when she twisted and pushed her nipple, tight and hard, into his palm. He held her like this, almost horizontal, one arm supporting her back, the other playing with her breasts, exulting in the response he knew he could elicit in her.

But then she sucked in air and shrank away, her mouth stilling under his. When she opened her eyes he could see the battle she waged, need versus denial. Self-denial.

Jordan swallowed audibly. "Not here."

"Are you sure, Jordan?" He ran his thumb over her nipple again, loving it's proud texture.

Jordan closed her eyes and her mouth fell open on a

gush of air. "You can't…" She arched her back to press against his hand once more.

Nick bent his head and sucked at the pebbled peak through her sweater, hearing her whimper. He doubled his efforts when he felt her knee nudge in between his legs, stop, and rub again.

"I can," he whispered, raising his head. Still supporting her, he took his hand from under her sweater and placed it between her thighs.

She tensed and squeezed, her body stiffening.

Nick cupped her, feeling her damp heat. "We both know I can."

He took her mouth again, recognized her capitulation in the way she strained against him, the insistent push of her knee into his aching groin. He'd held this woman in his arms, practiced his seduction on her enough times to know she was fast reaching the point of no return.

To know he was, too.

But even as her arms came around his neck, as she sagged back onto the arm of the couch, her weight dragging him down with her, his brain kicked into a higher gear, sending messages he didn't want to hear right now. He tensed, listening to her breath come in gasps, feeling her fingers tugging at his shirt buttons.

Yes, he could take her right now, right here. He'd proved it. But that made it just another coupling that underlined the shallowness of this affair. He needed her to believe he felt more for her than just a quickie once a week, to wonder if he had real feelings for her. If that was his goal, he had to stop.

Now.

Groaning, Nick pulled back, tearing his mouth away. She stilled, clutching a handful of shirt and confusion and desire smoking up her eyes. He pulled her upright and removed his hand from between her legs. "You're right." His thought processes might be on target but his hands were unsteady and awkward as he tugged the hem of her top down. "Not here. Not now."

Jordan sank back onto the arm of the sofa, her breathing still labored. As she fussed with her clothes and hair, a deep blush crawled up her throat and face.

Nick sighed. He hadn't meant to embarrass her. "I didn't come here tonight to take you to bed."

Her eyes slid over him briefly, then she leaned forward and rested her elbows on her knees, studying her feet. Her hair gleamed, a sparkling curtain in the dim light. Nick reached out and stroked it, feeling ridiculously tender.

"Come out for a drink with me." He tugged on a long lock of silky hair. "Who cares what anyone thinks?"

She shook her head, not looking at him. "I can't go out for a drink with you."

"Because of our fathers? How long are we going to let two old men dictate our lives?"

"It's just not worth the hassle, Nick." For a moment there, he almost thought she sounded sad.

"I think it is," he argued, surprised at how stubborn he felt.

"Let's just stick to Fridays for now." She reached out and covered his hand with hers, looking at him beseechingly.

If she didn't care a little, wasn't secure in the knowledge that he cared a little, she wouldn't have looked at him like that.

Mission accomplished. At least, he'd given her something to think about. He couldn't afford to push too hard or force her to choose between family loyalty or him until he was assured of success.

His breath returned, along with the blood to the rest of his body. He checked his buttons—often an occupational hazard with Jordan's impatient fingers. "Next Friday?"

Jordan rose to show him out. "Shouldn't we at least change the time or place?"

She was obviously still wary about the photos she'd received but Nick wasn't worried. "It's just some eagle-eyed reporter sniffing around. If he'd meant business, there would be a photo of me leaving the hotel, too, or a blackmail note."

Besides, he paid the hotel handsomely for their discretion. Why improve the odds of discovery by going somewhere else? "Make it earlier, then. Two p.m."

Five

To heck with chocolate! Jordan took her mug into the kitchen and tipped the cold contents down the sink, then poured herself a glass of pinot noir. Frustration, confusion—she paced the floor restlessly, going over every minute of the last half hour.

The whole episode was an embarrassment, starting with him catching her in a stupid avocado, cucumber and milk-powder face mask—oh, very elegant! Her humiliation was complete once he touched her, kissed her. He'd said *she* was like a drug, but he'd lit her up so quickly.

Thank goodness he'd had the sense to stop. Nick Thorne was already commanding way too much of her mind lately. Not that she'd ever tell him, but she thought about him plenty outside the hotel room. Several times a week at least, and always with a shiver of erotic anticipation. And when she did, suddenly the days of the week until Friday were an interminable bore.

The last thing she needed was the memory of him here in her lounge, naked, making love to her.

She flicked through the TV channels in an attempt to banish that enticing vision. Although—Jordan turned off the TV—thinking about sex with him was safer than thinking about anything else with him. Confident she could hold him enthralled in the bedroom for a while longer, she determinedly crushed the hope that, someday, Nick might see her as more. Starting a relationship with sex gave her no room to maneuver. He would never take her seriously—no one did. Even her father, her biggest fan, considered her an ornament. Despite her best efforts to change her lifestyle and prove everyone wrong, it really was easier to accept the cynicism and get on with the job. But she had the right to protect her heart along the way.

Even so, she hugged the memory of his jealous face tightly to her all night long.

On Tuesday, she was nearly involved in an accident when a car pulled out behind her into the path of an oncoming car. Jordan thought little of it until she noticed the same gray car behind her ten minutes later. It followed her to the supermarket and then to her parents house. Bemused, she drove around the block a couple of times. The car followed. Jordan pulled up and opened her door. The gray car slowed and then sped up and turned the corner. As it streaked past, she saw a bullet-shaped dark head in dark glasses atop a pair of burly shoulders.

She tried to shrug it off. Like Nick said, probably just a nosy photographer.

But the strange feeling stayed with her. The next day, as she waited for the lift in her building, a giant of a man stepped out. He wore a black suit and dark glasses. His head was close-shaven. She couldn't see his eyes but something about his expression, the look he gave her, made her shiver. He turned as she passed him and did not take his eyes off her until the doors closed.

The hairs rose on the back of her neck at the intensity of the look he gave her. Even once inside her apartment, she couldn't shake the feeling. She drew the drapes, poured herself a soda, started on dinner, all the while berating her vivid imagination.

She was being silly. Was it the photos, or her fear that if she and Nick were found out, she'd have to give him up?

She'd always felt perfectly safe here. There was no designated doorman manning the entrance, although there was a building supervisor. The residents used a swipe card to get in, which, as Nick had proved with his unannounced visit on the weekend, wasn't foolproof.

On her way to the court next morning, she asked the building super if he'd noticed a big man in the building yesterday.

"Big man, suit, dark glasses?" Robert said, and she nodded, her stomach doing a weird slide.

"Not in the building but there was a bloke across the street for most of yesterday, either sitting in his car or leaning against it. Seemed like he was watching the building. I thought it might be a cop."

"What kind of car?"

"Mercedes. Silver."

Jordan had no idea what type of car had followed her yesterday but the difference between gray and silver was open to interpretation.

Grow up in a fishbowl and you get suspicious.

But later, she thought she spied the same car following her home. Quickly pulling into a space on the street, she went into the nearest coffee bar and ordered a drink. Sure enough, a couple of minutes later, the big man in the glasses entered. He ordered from the counter and sat down by the door, facing her. She stared over the rim of her cup, her heart thudding, watching as he opened the newspaper he'd brought with him and raised it to conceal his face.

Despite herself, she smiled, looking for peepholes in the paper. What did he want? Feeling like a regular Nancy Drew, Jordan decided to have it out with him. Anything was better than wondering and at least there were people around.

Draining her cup, she stood and marched over to his table, flicking the newspaper smartly. "Is this it?" she demanded in a loud voice. "The rag you work for?"

The paper lowered and the man stared up at her, ridiculously still wearing his dark glasses. "Sorry?"

"I want to know who you work for," Jordan repeated.

The man picked up the cup in his dinner-plate-size hands and sipped before lowering it again. "I'm just hanging, reading the paper," he said.

Jordan frowned. Why wouldn't he tell her? It would come out anyway. "Do you deny you have been following me all over town, watching my building, every move I make?"

The woman at the next table stared intently with that gleam of sly recognition Jordan was only too familiar with.

The big man leered at her, leaving her in no doubt that he was enjoying the altercation. "I have no idea what you're talking about, Miss Lake," he said insolently.

Jordan sighed. She was getting nowhere, except making a spectacle of herself. At least the guy knew he was rumbled and when his story—whatever it was—hit the headlines, she'd have her father roast the editor.

She shook her head in disgust. "Just leave me alone," she muttered and stalked out the door.

He must be a reporter, she reasoned as she got into the car. The only other possibility was an investigator and why would someone want to investigate her?

Nick's thunderous face when he'd turned up at her apartment entered her mind. Jealousy, unwarranted as it turned out, but what if he hadn't believed her about Jason?

Jordan laughed out loud at the thought he would go to any trouble to keep an eye on her. Ridiculous! They each had their own lives and there was no tie between them. Sparked by the delivery of the photos, her imagination had spiraled into paranoia, just another example of her attention-seeking personality.

Nothing further happened that week and by Friday, she'd forgotten it and arrived at the hotel at the new time of two p.m., very much looking forward to seeing him.

Usually Nick checked in and waited for her in the

room. She headed for the elevators but happened to glance at Reception where two men stood with their backs to her. A thrill of excitement jetted through her when she recognized one as Nick. Jordan hesitated by a tall potted plant and decided to wait until he'd gone up, just in case she was recognized.

She thrummed with anticipation. Maybe he was right about their increased exposure to each other in court. She'd felt his eyes on her several times today, like a hot caress, making her tingle, building her excitement.

As she watched, Nick turned away from the reception clerk and spoke to the man beside him. A big man, with shaven head, a prizefighter's body and dark glasses.

Jordan froze. It was him—coffee bar man! She was sure of it.

She barely noticed as Nick walked on toward the elevators. Her eyes remained glued to the man, who just stared after Nick until he disappeared behind the elevator doors.

She moved right behind the plant now, shaking her head to clear it. Stay calm…she needed to think this through. The sequence of events was only seconds and she went over each one in slow motion. Nick reaching for the keycard, talking to the smiling receptionist, turning away from the counter, pausing to talk to the big man beside him. And then walking to the lift.

The man now had his back to her and Jordan took the opportunity to escape. She drove home in a daze and let herself into her apartment. And then she began to tremble.

Could it be true? Was Nick behind a sinister campaign to unsettle her? Was he having her followed because he thought she was sleeping with Jason? She sat there for nearly an hour but peace of mind eluded her. When her phone rang, she answered it with a sense of ominous fatalism, remembering his face on Saturday night, the hard tone of his voice that she'd never heard before. *"You want him, Jordan?"*

But it was her mother to say Syrius had suffered a heart attack and was being rushed to hospital. Jordan ran, forgetting all about Nick Thorne. Just as she reversed out of her space, she noticed Robert, the building supervisor, waving out to her. Next thing, there was a huge bang and sickening crunch, so loud, she thought there had been an explosion.

Her heart racing in fear and shock, she checked the rearview mirror to see a gray car at the back of hers, its front passenger door crumpled. A gray car—it filtered through the funk in her mind and she looked wildly about for Robert. Her panic eased slightly when she saw him crossing the car park toward her. She pushed open her door, her veins flooded with adrenalin.

And just as she did, Nick Thorne alighted hurriedly from his dented car. His gray Mercedes.

She froze, her mouth dropping open, keyed so tight, she thought she might scream.

"Are you all right?" In two steps, he was beside her, his face full of concern.

"Just *what* do you think you're doing?" she demanded, curling her hands into fists by her side.

"Are you all right, Miss Lake?" Robert approached, his eyes wide.

She ignored him and stared at Nick's face, catching the tension that rolled off him in waves.

"Why don't you look where you're going?" he demanded. "You could have been hurt…"

"You hemmed me in on purpose," she fumed. "Why are you following me?"

"I came to see where you were. I waited for nearly an hour."

"You had your stooge to keep you company. Get this—" she flicked her hand disdainfully toward his car, "—out of my way. I'm in a hurry." Turning, she stalked back to her car and yanked the door open.

"Oh, no, you don't!" Nick skirted around the car and grabbed her arm.

Vaguely she heard Robert offer a protest but all she could see was Nick's furious tight-lipped face.

"I'm not hanging around waiting for you, Jordan. That's the second time you've stood me up. You'd better have a damned good reason."

She tugged her arm from his grasp, desperate to get away and be with her father. "You're following me, stalking me," she said loudly for Robert's benefit. "And I want it to stop."

She slid into her car but he barred her door from closing. "What are you talking about?"

"Keep away from me, Nick!" Her demand was almost a yell. She glanced at the doorman. "I have a witness and he'll back me up. You're stalking me and I want you to leave me alone."

She gave a mighty pull on the door but he held it firm. "Request granted, and gladly." His eyes glittered like the ice in his voice. "You have much too high an opinion of yourself, Jordan Lake."

With that, he slammed her door and swiftly made his way to his car, flinging a sour look at Robert, who backed off quickly. Then he gunned the engine and sped from the car park, leaving only the tinkle and crunch of glass.

The aftershocks hit Jordan in a series of hot waves. She laid her forehead on the steering wheel, trembling with emotion. Incredibly, her anger had vanished along with Nick, and although he hadn't denied following her, the confusion in his face confused her. But she didn't have time to worry about that now. She had to get to the hospital.

Robert tapped on her window. "Your taillight's broken, Miss Lake. It'll need seeing to."

She grimaced. "Later. Robert, was that the car you saw outside the building this week, the one with the big man in dark glasses?"

Robert shook his head. "No, ma'am. It was a Mercedes, but silver, not gray."

Six

At eight-thirty on Monday morning, Nick exited his office elevator to find his brother sitting on his assistant's desk. His black mood darkened even more. "What do you want at this time of the morning?"

Noting Jasmine's flushed and suddenly busy demeanor, it occurred to him that maybe Adam wasn't here to see him at all. Scowling, he strode on into his office.

He'd spent the whole weekend stewing about the fight with Jordan—not that he had any idea what it was all about. One minute he was eagerly anticipating their lovemaking after a week's abstinence. The next, spun into a rage when she didn't turn up. Her accusations in the car park outside her building floored him and he could still hear the anger in her voice when she demanded he stay away from her.

Well, she'd got her wish. He flung his briefcase onto the desk, glad he was finished with it. Now, at least, he wouldn't have to lie about being booked up every Friday afternoon.

He hadn't even taken off his jacket when he heard Jasmine's startled "Wait!" and looked up to see the subject of his thoughts stalking in through his door. She marched straight in and flung the newspaper in her hand onto his desk.

Nick froze, his jacket half on, eyes leaping eagerly to her face. Jasmine appeared behind Jordan. "Nick, I'm sorry."

"Excuse us, please."

Jordan stood tall, her cheeks pink, eyes blazing. "What the hell are you playing at?"

With effort, Nick tore his eyes off her face and glanced down at the "Stepping Out" page of the local daily, picturing Jordan leaving the hotel. A brief caption read "Jordan Lake takes a break from the court case between her father and Randall Thorne looking glam as always in her little black dress." It was the same photo as the one that had been sent to her home. So it was a newshound after all.

But what did that have to do with him? He looked up into her face. "What am I supposed to have done now?"

"Don't give me that," she fumed. "Having me followed, watched—badly, I may say. Your goon didn't even care that I caught him."

Nick stared at her, uncomprehending.

She huffed out an agitated sigh. "The same gorilla I saw you with on Friday?"

Shaking his head, Nick finished removing his jacket and draped it over the back of his chair. "Gorilla?"

"At the hotel reception."

He eyed her while unbuttoning his cuffs and rolling his sleeves up. He'd never seen her angry before last Friday. Two minutes ago, he hadn't cared if he'd never seen or spoken to her again. Now, treacherously, his whole being warmed at the sight of her, sparks spitting from her eyes, her haughty chin raised high and mouth plump with a sullen moue. Nick was dangerously close to enjoying himself. "Jordan, what possible reason would I have to follow you?"

"I want it to stop, Nick." She leaned forward and rapped on the newspaper. "Now even my mother is asking questions, thanks to this."

She thought *he'd* sent the photo to the papers? Completely bamboozled—and worryingly exhilarated with it—he bit back a smile. The clouds that had darkened his weekend vanished in her presence, but he was astute enough to discern that if he smiled, she would probably deck him.

So he looked her straight in the eye. "Why don't you sit down and tell me about it," he suggested, doing his best not to sound patronizing. "I'll order some coffee and we'll…"

"I don't want coffee," she blurted, "and I don't want

to talk. I just want you to leave me alone." She stabbed the air between them with her index finger.

Nick started, filled with concern. There was something very wrong here. She was close to tears, more upset than he'd realized. Glistening eyes, the tremble in her voice… "Jordan…" He stepped around the desk but she whirled and made for the door.

He saw red. She couldn't just leave without giving him the chance to defend himself. He strode after her, his fingers grabbing her arm as she yanked the doorknob. "Don't you walk away from…"

"Keep away from me!" She lifted her arm to shake him. The door flew open and there was Adam, standing close, blatantly eavesdropping. Several heartbeats went by while both of them glared at him. At least he had the grace to step to the side and look contrite.

With a little huff of disgust in Adam's direction, Jordan turned her head to Nick. "In fact, keep your whole family away from mine."

Randall Thorne chose that moment to walk out of his office, stopping dead when he saw Jordan.

Jordan's eyes narrowed, all trace of her heated passionate plea lost in cool disdain. "You'll be pleased to know," she addressed the room in general, "that you won't be required in court this morning. The case has been adjourned."

Nick shot a warning look in Randall's direction in case the old man smart-mouthed her again.

"My father had a heart attack on Friday," Jordan continued. "He had an angioplasty and is still in the hospital."

Nick exhaled and took a step toward her. "Jordan…"

"Don't you dare say you're sorry," she snapped and gave each of the men in turn a bitter, recriminatory look. "Just keep away from us."

She stalked to the elevator, pressed the button and left.

No one spoke for a long moment, all eyes on the elevator. Even Jasmine looked stunned. Nick turned and walked stiffly to his desk, trying to assimilate what just happened. She thought he was stalking her, trying to blackmail her? And her father—sympathy welled up. God in heaven, what more damage could his family inflict on hers?

Adam and his father walked in. "What was *she* doing here?" Randall Thorne demanded.

Nick gave him a narrow glance. "Her father? What do you think?"

Adam cleared his throat and sat. Nick decided not to look at him, guessing his brother had heard a little more than he was entitled to.

He sat and rubbed his face briskly. "Christ, a heart attack." He felt somehow responsible and he could see on Randall's face that he felt the same. "This has got to stop, Dad."

"What did I…?"

"This bickering and fighting between you and Syrius. I don't care if you never shake hands and make up, but no more, do you understand?"

"He started this…"

"No, you started the latest outbreak by taking that award off him. He just carried it on."

"I've been insulted and slandered for years by that man. I've been the soul of patience and tolerance because your mother begged me…"

Nick raised his hand sharply and his father's voice trailed off. Come to think of it, he was just in the mood for a family conference. His blood was pumping—frustration, indignation at Jordan's wild accusations and shock about her father. And, if he was honest, the zing he got every time he looked at her…

It was time he got a few things sorted out around here. "Dad, I want you to announce your retirement at the birthday party."

His father looked up in astonishment. "Next month!"

"You'll be seventy. It's time to go."

"I'm in good health—" Randall harrumphed "—and things aren't settled yet." He cast a sideways look at Adam.

Both brothers raised their brows at their father.

"Adam hasn't decided—"

"Yes, I have, Dad," Adam cut in quickly. "And I've told you repeatedly."

"You're not on the plane yet, my boy," his father rumbled. "I want both my boys here."

"It's not going to happen," Adam stated.

Nick studied his hands. At thirty-four, the managing director of this place in all but name, he was tired of being fed crumbs and kept hanging. Of his father constantly playing him off against his brother. Nick had to show he was strong and worthy of the position. Randall valued strength above all else.

"Let's have this out right now," Nick said, leaning

back in his seat. "Face it, Dad. Adam is not coming back to Thorne's."

His father's eyes bored into him. "He would if you needed him, if you asked him."

Nick inclined his head. "Maybe. But I don't and I won't."

A sly light leapt in Randall's pale green eyes. "You jealous of your brother, Nick?"

Nick clasped his hands together, a small smile tugging at his lips. "Not at all." He flicked a glance at Adam who had the same thoughtful expression he'd worn since walking in here. "He knows that. But if you keep pushing, you'll lose him to London for good."

Nick hoped not. Adam had always said he'd settle in New Zealand eventually but for now, the lure of the world financial markets was too strong.

His father turned to Adam.

"Nick has it in one," Adam said, preempting the next salvo. "I'm doing what I want to do."

Randall's thick silvery brows knitted together. "This company is my legacy to you both…"

Nick sighed. He'd heard it all before, many times. "Are you unhappy with my performance?" he demanded, leaning forward intently.

His father blinked. "Of course not. You're doing a fine job."

"Then step aside," Nick said quietly. "Give me the recognition I deserve for running this place in all but name for the last five years."

Randall got heavily to his feet. "And do I interfere?

No! Why can't you be happy with that until Adam comes to his senses, dammit?"

Nick eyed him steadily. "Would you be?"

He knew the answer to that. Randall was a pioneer of his time. The empire he'd started was now one of the top three financial lending companies in the country, with a triple-A international credit rating and branches in all the main centers. Randall Thorne had never played second fiddle in his life.

"Not even to fulfill your mother's last wishes?" Randall had turned to glare at Adam's dark head.

Oh, he was good, Nick thought with a grudging admiration. He'd used every excuse in the book over the last couple of years. The truth was, he liked to keep an edge. Didn't want anyone getting too comfortable, too secure in their positions. Randall liked nothing better than having everyone scurrying around currying favor, vying to please him.

The old man left the office with a heavy step.

Adam stirred only when the door had closed behind him. "Good performance," he said quietly. "You weren't bad, either."

Nick leaned back, exhaling. "Am I being unreasonable?"

"Not at all. It's not like he does anything around here anymore."

"And I don't have a problem with him dropping in as often as he likes. But this is my domain now, and he's encouraged me every step of the way. He can damn well follow through."

Adam nodded. "You'll get there. But," he stood and moved to the window, "you have options, Nick."

Nick joined his brother at the window, glancing at him curiously. They were very alike, same height and coloring, although Nick was broader. He took after his father in physicality while Adam had a touch more of Melanie, slightly finer of bone, sharper facial features and fuller lips. Nick used to call him a pretty boy when they were young. He absently rubbed his nose, remembering some epic fights. Pretty Boy could pack an impressive punch, even if he was smaller.

"Maybe I'm tiring of the traveling, the women, the excitement—or it's tiring of me." Adam grinned. "I'm setting up an entrepreneurial start-up company. Savvy people with big ideas apply for funding and mentorship, but it's not just another angel investment company. I'm thinking big—global—and with some big names behind me."

"You've been watching too much reality TV," Nick said drily, but it was an interesting notion and one he'd like to hear more about. "Who are your investors?"

Adam named several captains of industry and IT. "I have my eye on a couple of big names, investors who will bring expertise and notoriety, not just money. If all goes to plan, I'll be ready to roll in the new year. But I could use a good man here. New Zealand is ripe for this type of opportunity." Adam turned to him with a glint in his eye. "It's not that different to what you do here, except that most of your clients are retirees and farmers." He approximated a yawn. "Be in on the ground floor, new innovative ideas, the future of the country."

Nick smiled, welcoming an old memory. "Remember when Dad used to bring us here on Saturday mornings before rugby? I'd watch him, listen to him talking to clients, working them. For all he's a bit rough around the edges, he knew how to treat people."

"So do you." Adam shoved his hands in his pockets. "You're just more refined."

Nick returned to his desk and sat. "Thanks, Adam. I appreciate the offer, but like you, I'm doing what I want to do."

Adam nodded. "I know. I'm just saying, you have options." He started for the door, then turned back. "Are you going to tell me what is going on between you and the Lake girl?"

Nick involuntarily glanced at the photo in the paper. His assault on Jordan's affections had hit a temporary snag with her father's heart attack. She wasn't likely to view his advances with a friendly eye while Syrius was in any danger of leaving this mortal coil.

But it was still the best option open to him, especially in light of his father's intransigence. And she was more than just a roll in the high thread-count linen of a five-star hotel. Nick hadn't even started showing her how much more.

But she would be the first to know. Meeting his brother's curious gaze, he smiled. "Nothing," he said firmly. "Nothing at all."

"Yeah, right," Adam muttered skeptically and sauntered to the door. "See you later, big brother."

Seven

"This beautiful Marlborough Sounds property for three million dollars, going once."

Nick scanned the crowd for the flash of blue silk that would give her away. He'd caught glimpses only, which probably meant she was avoiding him. It was nearly the end of the evening and he had only just arrived in time for the big item being auctioned tonight. He'd planned it that way.

"Three million dollars going twice."

A few faces close to him turned and nodded, their expressions curious and friendly. This was a media-free event, in as much as a hundred or so of New Zealand's high society could be secret. The organizer had wanted it that way. If Reverend Parsons hadn't filled him in on

Jordan's full involvement in the charitable Elpis Foundation, he'd be pretty miffed at throwing away a king's ransom just to impress a woman.

"Sold to the highest bidder."

Strangely, Nick felt little emotion for the huge outlay. No doubt his conscience would prick him tomorrow, especially when Adam or his father found out, but it was his own money he was using.

The auctioneer appeared and led him to a discreet table upfront, but to the side of the sumptuous ballroom to allow the dancing to resume. A couple of acquaintances patted his shoulder or winked as they passed but he invited no further conversation. His goal was to see Jordan.

"Please sit, Mr. Thorne," the auctioneer invited. "Can I get you some champagne?"

"No, thank you. Could you fetch Jordan Lake for me, please?"

The older man's face leaped with surprise and anticipation, but he immediately bowed his head. "Certainly. Feel free to look over the sale documents."

For the last three days, Jordan had refused to return his calls and after her performance in the car park, he was reluctant to go to her address. This morning, a wealthy client let slip that she was attending a charity auction for the Elpis Foundation. Nick recalled seeing the name in Jordan's apartment and that Russ Parsons was involved.

While he waited, he flipped through the pages of the Purchase agreement and assorted documents. Even with the real estate photographer's skill, the property looked shabby. The ad said the lodge was built at the turn of the century and still retained its "old-world charm"—another way of saying dilapidated. For one brief second, he wondered what the heck he was thinking.

But then he smelled her perfume, heard the swish of silk and the uncertainty of her voice when she spoke his name.

Nick got to his feet and stared at her for so long that the auctioneer who'd accompanied her backed off quickly. Jordan sat down stiffly.

She looked absolutely incredible. If he could recapture this moment in his mind forever and a day, he would recall every detail: the shade of her dress that matched her eyes—and the blue diamonds at her ears, he thought with a stab of triumph. Her glorious golden hair piled high with ringlets coiled around her face. The exact shade of pale pink lipstick as that which graced her fingernails, and her toenails, if he remembered correctly. The dress was a dramatic sheath of crisp silk, strapless, with a split bodice that emphasized her bust and cinched in her waistline. She was every inch the princess.

"You look lovely, Jordan," he said simply.

"Thank you. I'm—surprised to see you."

"Didn't Russ tell you? I asked him for an invitation, since mine obviously got lost in the mail."

"I didn't realize you knew him," Jordan said, smoothly ignoring his dig.

"My mother has always attended his church. He was a regular visitor to my parents' house during her illness."

Russ couldn't have been more enthusiastic with his endorsement of Jordan's many virtues. Tonight's glittering shindig she'd organized on the smell of an oily rag, begging favors all over town. Nick learned that she'd set up the Elpis Foundation with her own money a year ago. He heard all about her volunteer work at a free medical clinic and numerous other projects she had initiated.

And about her refusal to have her name associated with any of it. That interested him most of all.

He realized he was still gazing at her face when she shifted and cleared her throat.

"If you'd like to sign the contract…" she said with a pointed look at the papers on the table.

Nick sat down, giving her a smile that didn't quite reach his eyes. "Just as soon as you have the last dance with me."

She shook her head, confirming that she didn't trust him an inch—or was she worried about being seen with him? He observed that no one was paying them any attention. The orchestra was two minutes into the feisty *Die Fledermaus* and they were mostly obscured by the throng of dancers moving around the floor.

He faced her and leaned forward. "Come on, Jordan, do all your stalkers throw away a couple of mil just to impress you?"

She gave him a guarded look. "Some of my father's closest friends are here."

"I've just topped your sales for the evening. He'll understand."

"He's not well," she retorted. "And anyway, this isn't the last dance."

"Good, then you have a few minutes to explain why you think I've been stalking you."

Jordan sighed, staring moodily into the dance crowd. "You know why. The silver car. The big burly man with dark glasses, watching my building and following me everywhere." She picked up the pen, turning it over in her hands. "He gave me the creeps, staring at me all the time."

Nick decided not to point out that any red-blooded male in the world would have to be blind not to stare at Jordan Lake, especially tonight. "For someone who's made a career out of spicing up the gossip pages, you seem a little tense about some old photographer."

Her brows knitted in irritation. "It wasn't a photographer. I confronted him when he followed me into a coffee shop and he denied it—why would a newsman do that if his paper is about to run a story?"

Nick shrugged, skeptical. "What made you think I had anything to do with it?"

Jordan hesitated. "I—I remembered how you looked when you came around that night, when you thought I'd been with Jason."

"How I looked?"

She flushed prettily. "Angry. Jealous."

Nick leaned back in his seat. "And I don't have the right to be jealous, do I?" He knew he didn't. He'd given nothing of himself to this relationship, such as it was.

She looked down at the pen in her hands.

"I swear to you, Jordan, I had nothing to do with anyone following you. I was as invested as you were to keeping our meetings under wraps, especially with the court case going on. What possible reason…?"

Jordan took a deep breath. "Okay, I might have been

prepared to admit I was wrong about your involvement. And five minutes before I hit you in the car park…"

"Rammed me," he injected drily.

"You hemmed me in," she retorted. "I'd just been told of my father's heart attack. But it was seeing you with the man in the hotel that really spooked me."

"Back up. You went to the hotel on Friday?" He cast his mind back to Friday, a roaring of anticipation in his ears, fading with each passing minute, then an hour. The black rage of frustration that had him speeding over to her apartment building to have it out with her.

"Of course." She sounded surprised he would even doubt that. "I wouldn't let you down without calling."

He shook his head, confused. "I wasn't with anyone at the hotel."

The arch of one perfectly sculpted brow confirmed her skepticism. "I'd just walked into the lobby when I saw you talking to a man. You were both standing at Reception."

Nick started to deny it but her raised hand stopped him. "It was the same man, Nick. I got a great look at him in the coffee bar."

"I just picked up the key card…" Nick began, and then a memory kicked his indignation into touch.

"You were talking to him," Jordan insisted, "and then you walked to the elevators and he just stayed there, staring at you."

Nick remembered an insignificant detail. "Someone asked me the time." His mind had been so full of Jordan, he'd barely noticed the man who stood at the reception desk while he checked in. He hadn't given it another thought but in hindsight, it was a strange request considering the hotel wall behind reception had about a dozen clocks, all displaying time zones from around the world. "That was it. I told him the time and walked away."

Maybe this was something to be uneasy about after all. "Are you sure it was the same man, Jordan?"

"Yes."

"Perhaps you should call the police," he told her. "It's probably nothing, just a photographer hoping for a story, but just to be on the safe side…" He didn't want to spook her but she'd described quite a catalog of incidents. Some of it could be imagination, some less likely.

"The photo in Monday's paper was the last straw," she said gravely. "I thought you were playing some sick game."

"So you stormed into my office." No wonder she was rattled, and with her father's heart attack coming on top… He leaned forward again, resting his arms on the table. "Jordan, do you believe I had nothing to do with any of that?"

Jordan gazed at him for a long moment. She wouldn't describe herself as a great judge of character but she could see only concern and sincerity in his face—exactly what she wanted most to see. The past few days, she'd been miserable, hoping against hope there might be an alternative explanation.

His eyes reassured, soothed, seemed to see deeper into her than anyone had before. She nodded. "Yes. I'm sorry. It was just a weird couple of days."

The master of ceremonies announced that Strauss's *Wine, Women and Song* was the last dance of the evening. Nick stood and extended his hand. She rose, looking around nervously, but when he enfolded her hand in his and gave a reassuring squeeze, her reservations about her father finding out seemed trite. The man had made an enormous boost to the fund-raising coffers tonight. It would be surly to refuse him a dance.

She wanted to trust him. She'd trusted him with her body for months, and now her fears seemed silly. That aside, he was still the son of her sick father's oldest enemy. And she was afraid of risking her heart to someone who would tire of her soon enough.

They joined the other dancers on the floor and as the first notes rang out with military drama, the men bowed low to their partners. There was a lengthy introduction but at least this waltz was one of the shorter selections tonight. Jordan stood stiffly, waiting for the waltz steps to start and Nick moved close and put one big warm hand on her back.

And then she forgot everything, lost in the music she loved, the million double-quick turns and jaunty steps that he seemed to know as well as she. Jordan was a student of waltz for many years and liked to think she had inherited some of her mother's grace and ability. Nick moved well, full of confidence and purpose. Like he did everything, she thought wryly. But of course, his mother had been an outstanding dancer and teacher, too.

The music swirled, lifting her spirits, and she followed his commanding lead in perfect synchronicity, thrilled to find such a capable partner. Nothing beat the rapture of a fast Viennese waltz when two capable participants clicked on the floor.

Well, almost nothing…Nick rarely took his eyes from hers and she could see he, too, enjoyed the self-imposed discipline of being this close and yet perfectly proper. The teasing brush of his thighs, the masculine pressure of his hand at her lower back, the flat of his palm upon which her fingers rested, it all merged into a dance of restraint. How she knew was a mystery but she sensed how much he wanted to pull her close, mold her body to his. His hand wanted to close around her fingers, his other, to stroke up her back. That he managed to convey all this without a word was testament to their undeniable physical connection.

She sighed and tore her eyes from his. If the last week had shown her anything, it was that she'd become too vulnerable where he was concerned. It seemed Nick could elicit all sorts of wants and needs that she had no idea she was missing.

"Whoops, did I miss a step?"

He'd misinterpreted her sigh. She shook her head. "You dance well," she told him as the dance concluded and everyone ringed the floor and clapped the orchestra.

"My mother was determined that Adam and I could hold our own on the dance floor." He put a hand under her elbow and led her back to the table, his eyes suddenly troubled. "I'm sorry. It can't have been easy with your mother in a wheelchair."

Jordan was touched that he'd remembered, that he

cared enough, felt bad enough on his father's behalf, to mention it. "She supervised. We often watched videos together of her and your mother, the competitions."

"They were quite something," Nick agreed, pulling out her chair. But Jordan remained standing, somehow feeling she had more power that way.

How charming he could be. How strange that in nearly half a year's acquaintance, she was only just finding that out now. Not that he'd ever treated her with anything but respect, but what was his game now? What did he want from her?

The more she saw of this new Nick, the more she was being drawn in, but it couldn't be. Not now, not ever. He would find her out, find her wanting if he dug beneath the surface. And by then, she would be hopelessly in love.

And her father was ill, seriously ill. She couldn't add to that. She raised her chin. "Thank you, Nick." Picking up the pen, she held it out to him.

Nick glanced at it and then back to her face. "Am I being dismissed?"

"I have things to see to." She had to be strong, had to resist him.

He took the pen but made no attempt to use it. "You do believe that I had nothing to do with any of that last week?"

She held his gaze. "Yes. I believe you." Silently, she implored him to sign the paper. Leave while she still had a hope of saying no.

Nick's eyes bored into her, glinting with comprehension and disappointment. "This isn't over, Jordan. I want more."

Maintaining eye contact and a casual tone when every cell in her body clamored to know how much more wasn't easy. "It was fun, but it's over."

He didn't move one facial muscle but his flinty expression warned her it wasn't over, not yet. "That's it? One dance for three million dollars?"

It was like a slap with a cold fish. Charming when things were going his way, but ultimately, out for what he could get. She summoned an icy look of her own. "Why, no. You get this lovely property in a beautiful part of the country. It's an excellent investment."

The corner of his mouth lifted but his eyes were cool. "There is a condition of sale. I want you to show me the property."

Her eyes widened. "An auction is unconditional…"

"You want it sold or not?"

Damn, damn, she'd made a huge tactical error, shot her bullets too soon. "Nick, you can't go back on your word. This is for charity."

He scowled. "Are you willing to risk a bird in the hand?" He turned his head, gesturing at the queue of people lining up for their coats, the catering staff clearing empty tables, the orchestra packing up. "The evening is over. I'm your only buyer—*potential* buyer."

Her heart sank. How could she refuse with three million dollars at stake? How could she ever explain the collapse of the deal to Russ? They were counting on this money. "Why are you doing this?"

He picked up the contract and folded it. "I'm waiting."

He had manipulated her with cold, calculating

finesse. That was bad enough but how would she handle going off into the middle of nowhere alone with him?

Was it him or herself she didn't trust?

She had no choice. "If you think we're just going to pick up where we left off…" she muttered furiously. "Your three million bought this—" her fingers flicked the folded contract in his hand "—not me!"

He raised his hands. "That's your choice. Nothing will happen that you don't want."

That was cold comfort. They both knew she was incapable of resisting him once he started touching her.

"Be at Aotea Marina at eight a.m. on Saturday."

Great. She'd have to spend the three-hour ferry trip pretending she didn't know him—not that she would be talking to him. "The ferries don't leave from Aotea Marina," she said testily.

"Aotea Marina. Eight a.m sharp," Nick said firmly and tucked the contract into his jacket pocket.

Eight

"Something wrong?" Nick asked from the wheel of the Liberte 1V luxury cruiser.

Jordan closed her cell phone, frowning. They were an hour out from Wellington and her phone had just died in the middle of a text. She normally got reception most of the way across the Strait on the big public ferries.

She looked up into his questioning gaze. "One of the girls in our Outreach program has gone missing. Russ wants us to keep an eye out for her."

Letitia was fourteen. She came from a large family who'd hit hard times. They were loving and kind people who qualified for the support the church and the Elpis Foundation offered—and they gave much.

But two nights ago after a fight with her parents over

a cell phone—Letitia wanted one and they couldn't afford it—she'd left home and hadn't been heard from since.

Nick grunted. "Probably just hanging with her friends."

Jordan hoped so. In fact she could remember running away to friends to cool off herself at fourteen. But there was little comparison between the places she'd hung out and the options open to a young girl alone on the streets of Wellington.

"She came out here a couple of weeks ago. We had a Working Bee."

"At the lodge?"

Jordan broke off a little of the fluffy croissant on the plate in front of her. Nick had promised her a decent lunch on the floating palace, but for now, she was making do with coffee and still-warm croissants. "We've had a couple. Mostly picking up rubbish around the place and pulling up old carpet. Letitia had a ball and hasn't stopped talking about it, according to her parents."

"And Russ thinks she might have come back?"

Jordan sipped her coffee. "I don't see how. She has no money for the ferry, or the water taxi from Picton."

Talk of the Working Bee reminded her... "Do you mind if I bring back some stuff that we left last time? Some tools and food we were keeping for the next Working Bee. I'll bring it back today and get it out of your way."

He nodded briefly, but if he'd noticed the reference to coming back today, he didn't say anything.

Jordan had arrived at Aotea Square as instructed at eight sharp. Nick helped her aboard and then immersed himself in skippering the cruiser out of the harbor and into Cook Strait, that turbulent stretch of water linking the North and South Islands of New Zealand. He estimated the trip to their destination to be under four hours, plenty of time to make it back today.

And that was the only option, as far as Jordan was concerned. She was still miffed at his strong-arm tactics to get her here but she would play along—for now.

"Why were you holding Working Bees there when you intended to auction it off?"

"I hadn't intended to sell it at that stage. I'd planned to develop a retreat for families who never seem to have enough money to take a holiday." She felt her cheeks color. The idea seemed to have merit at the time she'd purchased the lodge, but in the cold light of day… "It was a pipe dream." She lifted her shoulders carelessly.

"Why?"

Jordan glanced at him. Nick looked like he was born on a boat. He wore tan chinos, moccasins without socks and a casual white shirt that he'd left untucked. A world removed from his suits and crisp business shirts. The breeze ruffled his dark hair, spinning it with dark gold tips. With the backdrop of the sparkling sea, his hands strong and capable on the wheel, he was master of his destiny.

And she'd do well to stop admiring his physical attributes and remember that she was here under duress. "I hadn't thought it through. Needy people don't want a holiday, they want tangible support, support they can see in their wallets and on their table. I meant well, but…" Jordan had no idea, really. How could she with her upbringing?

Nick frowned. "Doesn't sound like such a bad idea to me. Is it only the well-heeled who deserve holidays?"

"No, of course not." She lapsed into silence, feeling foolish.

"Why did you change your mind?"

"The big boy toys were a bit light."

He raised his brows.

"The auction," she qualified. "We expected a few more high-value items to put up for the charity auction. When they didn't eventuate, I thought the property might provide a draw card and fetch a good price for the coffers."

"Did you get what you hoped for?"

More time with you? The thought popped into her brain with the speed of light. That was how it had turned out but Jordan knew that wasn't what she needed. She merely nodded.

"Why all the secrecy, Jordan? Most women in your position can't wait to let the world know about the good works they do."

She knew that, but she'd also had a lifetime of people looking down on her because she was rich. "It's better that way. No one takes me seriously but this—the Foundation—is a serious business. The minute people realize that I'm involved, a lot of the support would dry up." She looked at him candidly. "For example, did you see an amusing headline about me three weeks ago? The Penny-Pinching Million-Hair-ess!"

Nick nodded. "Something to do with buying up shampoo on special."

"A woman took a picture of me with half a dozen

bottles of cut-price hair products in the supermarket. Neither she nor the rag she gave the photo to bothered to find out that I'd bought them for one of Russ's jumble sales. I often do things like that, but maybe I should cover myself in sackcloth and ashes."

"That would be a crime," he quipped, but there was genuine sympathy in his face.

She turned away from it. "I brought it on myself, the way I behaved—used to. People don't want to see me as anything other than a rich bitch."

"You're being too hard on yourself," Nick commented. "It's a lot more than most people are doing."

He was right, she supposed. Pity it had taken her so long to get a conscience.

"Tell me about Elpis. It means hope, doesn't it? Something to do with Pandora's box?"

"Technically, it was a jar," Jordan murmured, surprised at his interest. "A curse given by Zeus to punish mankind. It was entrusted to Pandora and when she opened it, all the good spirits were lost to mankind, except for hope." She shrugged self-consciously. "Something like that, anyway." Russ's interest in Greek mythology had inspired the name.

"And you set up the Foundation, financed the lot?"

Jordan nodded. There were no prizes for guessing what was going through his mind, that it was Thorne commercial real estate her trust fund was built on. Paid for by his father, so ultimately him. "Yes, it was from the trust fund that came from your father's land. But I think you know that."

"Do you think I'm after reclaiming that money, Jordan?" His tone was casual, his long considering look anything but.

She searched his face for hidden meaning, liking his directness. "No."

"Do you feel guilty about it? Is that why you give it away?"

That had occurred to her before. She had plenty of money apart from this particular trust fund. What had spurred her into suddenly developing a philanthropic streak a year ago, when this fund matured? "Do *you* think I'm guilty?"

It took a while but when it came, his smile was warm and melted her insides. "Guilty of being too good and too hard on yourself, maybe."

Too good? She wondered if anyone, especially her father, would see it that way if her torrid affair with Nick Thorne was discovered. "I'm no angel. I just have too much time on my hands."

"Did you never have any plans or ambitions of your own?" he asked.

Jordan liked art, which played right into her indulgent father's hands. A hobby rather than a career choice. "Daddy didn't exactly imbue me with a good work ethic." The sad thing was that Jordan had let him get away with that for so long. Taking his handouts, indulging in every pleasure, pleasing herself.

"Surely he could have set you up in one of his businesses somewhere."

She laughed out loud. "He doesn't believe in women

GET 2 BOOKS

We'd like to send you two *Silhouette Desire®* novels absolutely free. Accepting them puts you under no obligation to purchase any more books.

HOW TO GET YOUR
2 FREE BOOKS AND TWO FREE GIFTS

1. Return the reply card today, and we'll send you two *Silhouette Desire* novels, absolutely free! We'll even pay the postage!

2. Accepting free books places you under no obligation to buy anything, ever. Whatever you decide, the free books and gifts are yours to keep, free!

3. We hope that after receiving your free books you'll want to remain a subscriber, but the choice is yours—to continue or cancel, any time at all!

EXTRA BONUS

You'll also get two free mystery gifts! (worth about $10)

FREE!

If offer card is missing, write to Silhouette Reader Service, P.O. Box 1867, Buffalo, NY 14240-1867 or visit www.ReaderService.com

BUSINESS REPLY MAIL

FIRST-CLASS MAIL   PERMIT NO. 717   BUFFALO, NY

POSTAGE WILL BE PAID BY ADDRESSEE

Silhouette Reader Service
PO BOX 1867
BUFFALO NY 14240-9952

NO POSTAGE
NECESSARY
IF MAILED
IN THE
UNITED STATES

working. How he gets away without sexual discrimination charges for the lack of female employees—especially in the corporate sector—is beyond me." She glanced at him sideways. "And you are the very last person I should have shared that with."

Nick gave her another of his long, assessing looks. "I'm on your side, Jordan."

Her heart sank because something in her knew he spoke the truth. Suddenly his words at the ball the other night—I want more—took on ominous meaning. This wasn't just about sex or resuming their previous relationship. Somehow, for whatever reason, Nick Thorne wanted something more from her. And that was going to cause her heart all sorts of problems.

Jordan stayed silent, pretending he hadn't said that.

"You never wanted to get away, strike out on your own?"

"I'd miss Mom too much." That was a little twist on the truth. Syrius was a social animal whereas Elanor preferred home life. It was common knowledge he'd had a mistress for several years, but his wife and daughter always came first. The fact was, her mother would be more alone than ever if Jordan left Wellington.

It was a beautiful day with none of the bad weather and big seas that Cook Strait was famous for. Jordan asked Nick how long he'd had the big boat. He told her this was a charter.

"I had something similar but sold it three years ago. I never seem to find the time these days."

"Will you take over from your father when he

retires?" She knew her father and Randall Thorne were similar in age. Her mother made noises about Syrius retiring but Jordan privately thought they'd haul him out of his office in a body bag. That he had no son to take over from him was a source of great sorrow for her father, and something he constantly alluded to as proof of Randall Thorne's sins.

"That's what I'm working on."

She wondered why he sounded so grim, but he didn't elaborate.

After awhile, Jordan explored the plush vessel, surprised at the level of luxury on board. The stateroom was lavishly furnished, the kitchen nearly as good as hers at home, the bathrooms and hot tub inviting. To her surprise, she found two big cabins, both with beautifully decked out queen-size beds.

Jordan fully intended to ensure they got back to Wellington today but it was comforting to know she had a choice.

They weighed anchor in an inlet at the very tip of the Marlborough Sounds with the lovely name of Curious Cove. True to his word, Nick provided a fantastic picnic of chewy focaccia bread, tedaggio cheese, cold meats and crayfish. For dessert, there was a warm blackberry tart. There was wine, too, but Jordan declined, feeling she needed a clear head about her with Nick around, especially when he wasn't drinking.

After lunch, they made their way through the beautiful bays leading to the famous Queen Charlotte Sound, and finally they arrived at the jetty that led to the lodge.

"Don't expect too much," Jordan warned as she packed away the food while he prepared to tie up the boat. "No one has lived here since it went out of business seven years ago. The owner died, someone in the family contested the will and it's been tied up in an estate wrangle till I bought it two months ago."

The jetty was quaint but serviceable, but Nick's smile faded fast when confronted with the deteriorating facade of the house. Weatherboards missing or rotting away, crying out for a lick of paint, broken windows…

She quickly drew him away from the spot where the veranda sagged alarmingly, handing him the keys before he bolted.

"How often have you been here?" he asked dazedly.

"Three or four times, twice with the Working Bee." There was a tense moment when she wondered if he'd actually rip up the contract before setting a foot over the threshold. The old house was in terrible condition, but there were some lovely features inside and the setting made up for it.

They spent the first hour on the upper level and discovered the three bathrooms needed serious remodeling and plumbing. The seven bedrooms were dated but dry and she noted a little more enthusiasm from Nick when he saw the views they had to offer. From every window, hills toasted by the sun gave way to slopes of dense dark green forest, rising out of the network of sparkling waterways.

Then it was downstairs to the three living areas. There was a huge room that could almost have been a ballroom, complete with some lovely leadlight windows, all of which seemed to be intact. A smaller room with a conservatory boasted wonderful water views. Finally, the large open dining room with built-in rimu wood benches and tables, leading into the kitchen. The wallpaper was peeling, the paint on the kitchen cupboards too, but it was big and bright and airy.

Jordan moved into the kitchen, hoping their efforts last trip had eliminated the rodent problem. The large sports bag she'd left on the kitchen bench last time was open, a box of teabags sitting beside it with some of the contents spilling out onto the bench.

Funny, she could swear she'd packed everything away before leaving.

"I've seen something like this before," Nick called from the dining room.

Jordan looked up to see him gazing at the large bold mural on the wall.

She zipped up the bag, wondering which of the kids had nicked her large Tupperware container filled with biscuits.

"Something similar, anyway," Nick said, peering closely at the mural. "No signature."

Jordan felt no need to volunteer the fact that she was the artist. Drawing was just a hobby, not something she took seriously. She had been rained in on her second trip here, alone without the group. Sketching seemed a great way to pass the time, although she fully expected the wall to be painted over sometime soon.

Nick turned around. "This was in your apartment. Not this exact one," he gestured at the mural "but something similar. Same tone, a couple dancing." His face suddenly cleared. "*You* did this."

Jordan hoisted the bag. "Uh-huh." She wondered where to look for the other tools and paraphernalia the Working Bee had left.

"These are good," Nick enthused. "Do you sell them?"

"No. It's just a hobby." Jordan frowned at the sight of the old black kettle sitting on the bench. She thought she'd emptied it and set it on the gas cooker. She reached out to touch the kettle.

"How do you expect anyone to take you seriously if you don't yourself?"

Jordan didn't answer him because she was distracted by the warmth of the kettle. She spread her fingers on the belly of the vessel, frowning. "It's hot," she said, more to herself than him.

Nick came over to lean on the bench. "It's sitting in direct sunlight."

Right, and it shouldn't be. There were matches on the bench by the gas cooker. "I wonder...I could swear I packed everything in that bag before we left last time and zipped it up. And there's a big box of biscuits missing."

Nick shrugged, his interest waning. He wandered over to the huge open pantry, his nose wrinkling in distaste.

Jordan nearly smiled. Rodent droppings, perhaps, or a corpse in one of the many mousetraps she'd set.

There were no cups in the sink. If there was an intruder, they were house proud. "I'm thinking of Letitia, the missing girl."

"More likely to be a hunter or tramper. This is on the Queen Charlotte Track, isn't it?"

The Queen Charlotte Track was one of New Zealand's most popular tourist destinations, a seventy kilometer walk through lush subtropical native bush, showcasing the tranquil and stunning scenery of the Marlborough Sounds. Many thousands took to the track all year around.

"The door was locked," Jordan pointed out, unconvinced. The house seemed secure downstairs, but perhaps someone could access one of the broken windows upstairs from the crumbling exterior fire escape. She tried to call Russ to see if the girl had returned home but there was still no cell phone reception, even on Nick's phone.

"Atmospheric conditions." He shrugged.

They decided to explore the grounds. After all, that's what they were there for. But now they had an additional purpose: looking for Letitia.

They wandered the expansive and overgrown grounds for the next few hours. Nick wasn't much of a gardener but even he could see that under the neglect, this was a pearl of a property. There were treasures everywhere. Human faces carved into punga fern trunks, hammocks entwined with ivy, perishing between their supports, stone seats set in the most glorious positions to catch the late sun over the web of waterways and forested cliffs.

Jordan spotted a plastic wrapper; the brand of biscuits that were supposed to be in the Tupperware container in the kitchen. "It could have been there for ages," Nick cautioned, not wanting to get her hopes up.

"Our Working Bee went through here with forks and bags, picking up all the rubbish."

Perched on the hill behind the lodge was an old rickety chicken coop, the straw molding and smelly. And there was the empty Tupperware container, sitting in the corner.

"It *must* be Letitia."

Although Nick was skeptical, he accompanied her, clambering around the steep slopes and thick scrub high above the house, calling the girl's name.

No one answered their calls. Finally, Jordan looked at her watch and gasped with dismay. "Are we going to get home before dark?" He'd told her it was a condition of the charter that the boat be moored after dark.

"If you really think she's around here somewhere, then we'd best stay and have another look in the morning," Nick said casually as they started down the hill. "Besides, I hired the boat for two days."

Jordan stopped abruptly and turned her head. "Two days?"

Nick gazed at her unrepentant. Surely she didn't think this was just about sex, did she? His plan was to get her to himself for a while, away from the hotel room and the constant worry of discovery. He wanted to see if they clicked outside of the bedroom as well as they did in.

Anyway, this wasn't his fault. If she hadn't been adamant her runaway was here, they could have started for home two hours ago.

Jordan turned fully to face him, something close to

a pout on her lovely mouth. "And if I have plans for the evening?"

"Then he's going to be disappointed," he said evenly, absorbing the jolt he always got when she looked at him face on and close. The shape of her brows provided a perfect frame for those gorgeous almond-shaped blue eyes. Her luscious mouth with the prominent bow in the center just begged to be kissed. Beauty was in the eye of the beholder, he knew, and for Nick, he could never tire of looking at her face.

His body, too, rarely escaped the knowledge without a reaction of some kind. His mouth dried, his stomach muscles tensed. Every nerve ending sent an "I want" message to his brain.

"I didn't bring anything with me," she said curtly. "Clothes. Toothbrush."

"There are spare toiletries on board. As for clothes…" His gaze swept over her white top and long white shorts and sneakers. It was too late for them, streaked with dirt and plant matter. His own weren't much better. "I think there are robes in the bathrooms," he said innocently. Clothes were optional for what he had in mind…

Her eyes narrowed as if she read the path of his thoughts. "Well, that's worked out nicely for you, hasn't it?"

She was right, it had all worked out perfectly. The missing girl situation was an unexpected stroke of luck.

Still, he didn't want her sulking all night. "We'd have finished exploring the gardens two hours ago—plenty of time to make it home before dark—if we weren't looking for your friend," he reminded her. "Jordan, you have options. There's enough food and wine for dinner, I think. And there are two cabins on board, as I'm sure you noticed."

Nick wanted this chance for her to get to know him. It would take a major leap of trust for her to consider a public relationship with him while her father was ill. But if she thought he was really into her…Randall and Syrius had to be persuaded that further offenses would hurt their children.

As he watched her struggle with the desire to keep a cool distance between them, Nick knew he was getting under her skin. She could dictate the time frame and boundaries—to a point—but he would use the irresistible sexual connection between them to achieve his goal.

Nine

They searched the house once more, then locked up and walked back down the jetty to the boat. Jordan rubbed her arms briskly. "I hate to think about her all alone out here."

"If she's here, she'll know we're looking for her," Nick reassured her. They'd yelled themselves hoarse. "She'll come down to the boat when she gets cold or hungry."

Together they prepared a salad and the leftovers of their lunch. Nick had brought pre-baked rolls which they warmed up in the small oven in the galley. He opened the wine, his eyes following Jordan as she moved around setting utensils and crockery on the table, lighting candles. He wanted her more with each passing second, but tonight was going to be her call all the way.

The meal was simple, enhanced by the wine and the candles she'd lit. The reheated blackberry tart tasted even better than at lunch. They got through it all with an easy rapport, the wine mellowing her initial reticence.

"This is a novel experience," he commented as they finished. "Sitting across a table from you, eating and talking."

"We did that at lunchtime," she reminded him.

Nick pushed his dessert plate aside. "Will your father be in court on Monday?"

"If the doctor is happy." Jordan paused then rolled her eyes resignedly. "I spoke to him yesterday and he was looking forward to it."

"You know he's going to lose, don't you?" He wasn't being confrontational. There was little doubt about it.

Jordan nodded. "We've all told him but he's too stubborn to accept it."

"What's he like?"

She smiled fondly. "Impossible. Everything is black or white with him. He has an opinion on everything and I don't think he has ever been persuaded to change it, even in the face of irrefutable evidence."

"And you're crazy about him." Nick wondered if one day her eyes would mist with emotion for him.

"There's being crazy about him and there's driving me crazy."

Their eyes and smiles met and tangled but curiously, every time they did, Jordan would take a sip of wine. Her nervousness was unexpected.

She sat across from him in a decidedly grubby top,

her ponytail slipping and a twig in her hair. Used to seeing her light up the tabloids in designer clothing that flattered her magnificent body—or alternatively, naked on Fridays—Nick warmed at the sight of her. The sparkle in her eyes could be put down to the wine or candlelight, but he hoped he may have contributed there in some small way.

Operation Jordan was under way. "It must have been unreal growing up in that mansion as an only child." The Lake mansion in Kelburn was infamous for its grandeur.

Jordan relaxed back into her seat. "I think there was a friend roster. I don't recall being lonely at all."

"Spoiled rotten," Nick grinned. "The biggest and best birthday parties…" The ostentatious celebrations were legendary in Wellington society.

"They were insane! Clowns, animals, costumes, so much cake and sweet stuff that we'd all get hyper…the tantrums when it was all over!" She gave a mock shudder. "My poor mother. I'd make myself physically sick with the excitement of it all!"

Jordan picked up her glass again. He was going to have to carry her to bed at this rate.

He stood, picked up the bottle and topped her glass off, smiling at her. While he was there, he pulled gently at the twig tangled in her hair, handed it to her and then went back to his seat.

"It's interesting," he said as he sat. "You have the whole world at your beck and call and yet you hide behind some foundation, too scared to show yourself.

You don't want anyone to know that you have values and talent."

"I know I have those," she said, lifting her shoulders in a careless shrug, "but it's the money that makes the difference, that differentiates me from anyone else."

Nick laughed. "I must be wearing rose-colored glasses then because from where I sit, I see something else entirely."

Jordan didn't respond, toying with the twig he'd handed her.

But Nick was interested. She seemed to have everything a young woman could want. What was she afraid of? "Gorgeous," he began, smiling again when she frowned, "Talented as I can attest to, having seen some of your art…"

"Drawings," she interjected.

"Art," Nick went on, heedless. "Proactive—you're doing something that makes a difference to a lot of people."

"Lots of people do that…" She snapped the twig in half and laid it on the table, looking at it as if it personally offended her.

"Probably, but they don't hide it. Did I mention creative? That ball the other night was a work of art, if I'm any judge of things."

"You think putting on a party makes you an artist?" she asked innocently, but sarcasm laced her tone.

"Don't knock it. People go to college to learn that stuff. The skills required get you a diploma. You just get on with it and make it happen."

"Because of my money." She insisted, nodding vigorously. "Do you honestly think I would have put together that ball without my father's influence and contacts?"

She sat back as if she'd won the argument.

"The difference, Jordan, between you and most rich people is that you use your money, you do something useful with it."

"Oh, I've frittered away a lifetime of money, believe me."

"I believe you," he said, grining, "but take some credit for making up for it now."

"What was your childhood like?" she asked, twisting the stem of her glass, moving the focus from her.

"Pretty normal. School. Rugby. Sailing. A few family holidays."

"Were you close?"

Nick had no complaints about his upbringing. "Adam and I were—are—I suppose. Mom and Dad—we got on all right. They weren't very demonstrative and they were always so busy with their respective careers. Dad liked to pit me and Adam against each other all the time. Everything was always a competition." He rolled his eyes. "Still is, far as Dad's concerned."

"Who won?"

"It was about sixty-forty. I was bigger but preferred negotiation. Adam liked to pretend he was David to my Goliath."

Her smile faded as she gazed into his eyes over the candlelight. Nick nearly groaned aloud. She was killing him here, so damn beautiful, so desirable. The sexual chemistry between them was a palpable pull, one he wasn't used to tamping down. That was the main disadvantage of starting as they had started—having to exercise self-control.

But he had to, just for a while longer. Until she accepted that what they shared was worth the fire and brimstone their fathers would rain down on them.

The moment lay between them like a suffocating cloud of fizz-edged awareness, stretching for long seconds.

Finally she looked away, frowning. "I was trying to imagine you as a boy."

Yeah, right, Nick thought. She was wondering why he hadn't moved, leaped across the table, pushing and demanding as he usually did when she looked as him with naked desire in her eyes.

Your move, baby.

The silence lengthened as they stared at each other, rocking gently in the swell of the waves lapping the jetty.

What was the deal? Jordan wondered. Didn't he want her anymore?

Nick's smile was strained at the edges, his eyes feverish with want. She recognized that because she saw it every Friday when he opened the hotel door to her.

Yet he sat there, one hand spread on his thigh as he lounged in his seat, the other on the table. Looking at ease and yet ready to pounce.

Why wasn't he pouncing? He always made the moves. In the time it took for them tonight to prepare dinner, eat and then have a nice little chat, they would normally have made love two or three times.

Was it a test of some kind? Jordan shifted in her chair, a meter away from a man bristling with sexual tension and yet concealing it—not even that. Accepting it.

What was his game?

She stood abruptly, needing some space. "Do you mind if I take a shower?"

He moved his head from side to side, his eyes hooded.

Jordan made her way to the small bathroom off the second cabin. True to his word, there were unopened toiletries, toothbrushes in their wrappers and a stack of soft white towels on the vanity. She turned the shower on and scrutinized her grubby clothes. After clambering around a dusty house and up cliff and vale, the white lacy top was a shambles and the cutoffs weren't much better. She stripped and took the top and her panties into the steaming shower with her; the cutoffs wouldn't dry before morning.

The hot blast of water was bliss after a long day. She'd drunk too fast. Nervous. He made her nervous because he was different. Holding back, even though every look told her he wanted her. The only conclusion she could make was that he wanted her to make the moves. But why?

She turned and let the water pummel her back while squeezing shower soap through her clothing. It was all so confusing. At the ball, she'd told him it was over. Now she wished they could return to sex on Fridays, where they both knew where they stood. Two unattached people sharing an amazing attraction.

That reminded her of what he'd said at the ball. *"I want more."*

She turned off the shower and grabbed a towel. Did she want more? Of course she wanted more. The idea grew and grew until it pushed everything else out of her head. More with Nick than Friday afternoons. Dating Nick. Making love with him in her apartment, his house. Talking about their day. Making plans.

She had drunk too much to be thinking along these lines. The prudent thing to do in the circumstances was to poke her head back into the saloon, wish him good-night and go to bed—alone—in the second cabin.

She rubbed the steamed mirror with a corner of the towel. Looking at herself, her naked body, reminded her of when he'd made love to her in front of the mirror at the hotel. She could see him behind her, his dark hands on her white breasts, his face above hers, eyes holding hers fiercely, compelling her to watch…unmentionable pleasure coiling through her body as he moved inside her, came with her.

Jordan flushed bright red. God, she was hot for him. He was addictive. She craved him. And trying to deny the craving, she began to justify herself. It was she who'd said they weren't going to pick up where they left off. Her rules, she could break them. Going meekly off to bed alone was going along with him, changing the direction of what was a great sexual relationship.

The best solution was to go out there and seduce him. Remind him that they were about sex. Remind him how good they were at it. Keep things on the only level she was prepared to contemplate. Because she didn't want to risk her heart, which she feared was already attached.

She dried herself, brushed her teeth and her hair, and hung her panties and top over the towel rail to dry. Then she went out to seduce Nick Thorne before he turned her head with his charm and his patience and his tests.

Jordan walked out into the stateroom wearing only a towel. He lifted his head and watched her approach, his eyes gleaming. She tried to pretend this was the Presidential Suite at the hotel on a Friday afternoon. She'd done this a dozen times…

He'd cleared the table and now sat on the sofa, holding his glass. "Shall I find you a robe?"

Jordan shook her head, confusion welling up again. Why wouldn't he just stand and take charge? Tear the towel off, put his hands on her…

"Would you like coffee?" His voice was so soft that she strained to hear him.

"Maybe later," she said huskily, moving closer. Her bare legs were just inches from where his stretched out in front of him.

"You want me, Nick?"

He moistened his lips. "You've never asked me that before."

"I've never had to."

He laid his head back on the back of the couch, watching her inscrutably. Never had she known him to exhibit so much restraint. Admirable restraint, considering the impressive bulge at the apex of his trousers.

Goose bumps rose on her arms and she shivered, the tension coiling up her insides.

"Remember our first time?" he asked suddenly, his

voice low and hard. "You trembled then, too, just like now. Were you nervous?"

She exhaled in a rush. "Just like now."

She hadn't meant to admit that.

She took a tentative step closer.

"Why?"

There was nothing in his upturned face she could read, no clue as to what he was thinking. "Because I was overwhelmed."

The back of her neck—her whole back prickled like freezer burn.

"And now?"

"Because I don't know what you want anymore." Jordan hadn't intended to say that either. But she couldn't think with his impenetrable eyes boring into her.

"I told you the other night," Nick said quietly. "I. Want. More."

Someone had switched scripts. She suddenly felt all at sea again—she nearly snorted but it wasn't funny. Desperate to regain the lead—wasn't that what he wanted?—she slipped her fingers between the folds of the towel, under the knot, peeling the sides back a little, slowly revealing what was underneath. "You can have everything."

Nick smiled then, as if to himself. "Oh, I intend to."

It sounded like a threat.

Firmly pushing her worries aside, she stepped inside his legs and sank down onto her knees before him. That got a result. Quickening breath, eyes widening and alert. The column of his throat bobbed in a hard swallow. *Got your attention now,* she thought.

She reached out and spread her hand on his groin, soaking up the heat that radiated out. The answering surge of welcome under her palm made her smile and she pressed down gently. "You want this?"

His chin dropped down to his chest. Nick always liked to watch.

"You know what I want."

She bent to her task, brushing off the niggling unease about his unaccustomed passivity, the way he answered her every question with a variation of "I want more." His arms were still, hands on his thighs, when usually he moved, directed, arranged her to his satisfaction.

Thankfully as she unzipped him, her natural instincts took over. Jordan was enthralled, turned on beyond belief. She didn't need to ask again. She knew by the fire in his eyes. The way the veins on his hands stood out, even though they appeared to be relaxed. The muscles in his upper thighs tightened with each swirl of her tongue around his swollen flesh.

She knew exactly what he wanted when she felt his hands in her hair, firmly holding her in place while he moved under her.

But then someone changed the script again. His hands tightened in her hair and he lifted her head and pulled her up over him.

Nick had never stopped her before.

It cost him. The strain on his face, a single bead of sweat crawling down his temple, told of the cost. He framed her face with his hands and kissed her, deeper and deeper, and it was somehow more intimate than her ministrations a minute ago. She felt heavy, dragged down by desire.

They kissed and kissed, cupping each other's faces, learning the shapes of their cheekbones and skulls, fingers lacing through hair. There seemed to be no urgency and neither of them closed their eyes. To Jordan, the sight of him was just so good.

His hands slid inside the still-knotted towel, stroked slowly down her body, massaging gently while they kissed. Lying on top of him, feeling him hard and wanting underneath her, she drowned in pleasure.

Maybe she'd begun by seducing him, showing him how sexy he made her feel, teasing him until he begged. But he was involved now, involving her completely, taking her under. She needed skin and squirmed to get her arms down, trying to get to his buttons. There was too much between them. She fumbled and tugged and got his shirt undone so at least she could feel his warm skin on her front, the hairs on his chest causing fantastic friction on her breasts.

Under her towel, he stroked and stroked, his hands questing and probing. She lay across him, lifting her hips. His fingers played her like music, inside and out, and she flowed into orgasm with blinding ignorance, not even realizing she was close. Her hands fisted, her knuckles pressing into his chest and for the first time since she'd walked out from the bathroom, she broke eye contact and sank into deep and shuddering satisfaction.

Soon, he slid out from under her, sitting her up, pulling her forward—this was more like it, she thought, taking charge, directing operations. All thought fled when he knelt in front of her and made love to her with his mouth.

Too sensitive to bear, she had nowhere to hide. Her hands plunged into his hair. She arched her back, fighting for breath that refused to come and then roller-coasted over her with a low keening sound that went on and on.

When it was over, she attempted to relax her stiff fingers from his hair, but it wasn't easy. "Yes," she said and her voice sounded a million miles away. The boat rocked gently on its mooring. "This. This is what I want."

Nick sat back and pulled his shirt over his head. Sated yet burning for more, she watched him strip and take care of protection. Then he pushed her down on the couch, moving purposefully over her and looked into her eyes.

"No," he said, matter-of-factly. "It's not all you want." He nuzzled her lips before raising his head again, his gaze triumphant.

She felt his tip nudge her, realized he was right.

"You just don't know it yet," he said in a voice that told her with certainty that the lesson was about to begin.

Her eyes flew wide as his hands moved up her forearms, pushing her arms above her head, lacing their fingers together.

She was tired of wondering and wanting. She just wanted him inside her. "Nick…"

He obliged. The blistering invasion, slow and strong, deep and relentless, filled her so utterly it forced the air from her lungs. He stilled, tense as a board, his hands pressing hers down into the sofa, forcing her to look at him. They gazed at each other for long seconds while he pulsed inside her, and Jordan understood. Never again could she not take this seriously. Never again could she think it was just sex.

Not just sex. Sex of the mind and body and soul. As he moved, slowly withdrawing and then sliding home again, imprisoning her eyes, she forgot everything but the wonderful warm rush of emotion that accompanied this act, this time.

Countless Fridays, countless orgasms, but never a bond so deep before. It shone from his eyes, so strong she turned her head but he wouldn't let her. It pumped through his body till she felt it in her womb and in the pulse beating through his fingers as they gripped hers. *I want more,* his eyes said as he moved, each deep thrust shattering her fears. "More," she answered him, exhilaration bursting through when he smiled down, warming her heart.

Drunk on it, she wrapped her legs around his waist as he plunged with consuming intent. The pace and intensity got crazy, the flashpoint poised, hissing, and then boiled over in a rush. He choked out her name once as she moaned her satisfaction. And she knew nothing could ever be desired again. The rush slowly ebbed. The thud of their calming breath and the occasional sound of small waves lapping the hull was all she could hear.

Still looking into her eyes, Nick slid his arms around her and held her, for the first time ever.

Ten

Jordan awoke slowly, in her customary manner. It took a few seconds to realize she wasn't alone, quite a few more to replay the night's events in her mind and think about how she felt, waking next to Nick.

They'd enjoyed many sexual adventures in the past, but last night easily qualified as the best night of her life. It was almost like a real date, spending the day together, making dinner together, talking. And then, the most emotionally-charged lovemaking she'd ever experienced. How could she even think of holding anything back? He wouldn't let her.

Nick stirred behind her with a contented growl. Jordan sighed, her erotic memories scattering. Moving an inch at a time, she began to edge toward the side of the bed but hadn't gotten far when his warm arm clamped around her middle.

"Morning," he mumbled.

Jordan mumbled a similar response.

"Where do you think you're going?" He shifted closer, his big warm body enfolding her back like a heated cloak.

She half-turned, craning her neck to see him. "Bathroom. I need to clean my teeth."

Nick lifted up on one elbow, blinking owlishly.

She squeezed her eyes shut. "You're not allowed to look at me until I've got my face on."

He tapped her on the nose until she looked at him. "I've seen you with the green goop, remember?"

Oh, God, how could she forget?

"You, Jordan Lake," he said gallantly, "don't need makeup to look beautiful."

She smiled into his eyes, thinking she could get used to waking up next to a sleepy, unshaven, tousled man whispering sweet nothings in her ear. But within seconds, his gaze sharpened and flared with heat. He shifted his body, imprisoning her under him and she felt his arousal, thick and hot against her thigh. The messages to her brain had nothing to do with vanity now.

How long before this wanes? she wondered, running her hands over his long, broad back and thickly-muscled arms? With one look, like the flick of a switch, he turned her on instantly. Her body responded, quickening, moistening. Would the time come soon when they could look at each other and resist succumbing to the most urgent and primitive desire?

Nick's hand slid under the small of her back, lifting and angling her hips, then bent and sipped at the corners of her mouth. She kissed back and decided to enjoy it while it lasted. "While we can both still walk," she murmured against his chin. He pulled back an inch, his eyes questioning. In response, she hugged him tighter, welcoming his advance, his slow, slick invasion. Welcoming him home.

An hour later, she was in the galley making coffee when she heard strange noises outside. Peeking out the porthole window, she saw her runaway sitting on the wooden jetty, hugging her knees to her chest and sniffing loudly.

"Letitia!" Jordan rushed out and sank down beside her. The poor girl sobbed with relief, nearly hysterical with nerves and cold. She wore scruffy dungarees, sneakers with no socks and only a thin hoodie.

Nick responded to her calls and they helped the teen aboard and wrapped her up in a duvet. It may have been late spring, but the sun hadn't made it over the valley yet and the air was crisp and cool. Nick set about making breakfast while Jordan sat with the girl, rubbing her frozen hands between hers.

Letitia had sneaked under the tarpaulin of a utility as it boarded the inter-island ferry in Wellington. She then walked from Picton to Anakiwa and linked up with the Queen Charlotte Track to get here, which had taken "at least a whole day." She'd eaten the biscuits and made cups of black tea from the provisions the Working Bee left in the old lodge kitchen. But the cold was her enemy.

"There was nothing to sleep in, not even any old curtains."

The Working Bee had disposed of all the moldy old drapes that had hung in the lodge for decades.

When Nick and Jordan docked, the girl hid, determined not to be discovered, but another night alone in the cold had changed her mind.

"Why didn't you answer our calls? You must have heard us." It occurred to Jordan that while she and Nick were making love here on the boat last night, this poor girl was frozen and alone. "You should have come to the jetty and called me."

Letitia wolfed down eggs and toast like she hadn't eaten in a week. Then Jordan tucked her up in the bed in the second cabin. "Poor kid," she said to Nick as they prepared to set off back to Wellington. "She just wants some attention. She's the youngest of six. Her older brothers are in and out of jail and her sister has leukemia. Her parents spend all their time either at the hospital or bailing the boys out. No one has time for Letitia."

Jordan couldn't comprehend that, coming from a one-child family, the apple of her parents' eye. She resolved to keep a much closer eye on the girl from now on.

"Told you so," Nick said lightly.

"What?"

"Sounds to me like that family needs a decent holiday, spend some quality time with their kids…somewhere nice and remote with fishing and tramping…"

Jordan felt her face color in pleased embarrassment.

He liked her idea after all. That meant a lot, even though it was no longer hers to develop.

They made good time on another amazingly calm day. After a couple of hours, Letitia appeared and helped Jordan cobble together enough leftovers to make some sandwiches. Then they sat out of the sun in the stateroom, leaving Nick on deck. Since neither had gotten much sleep the night before, it wasn't long before they stretched out on the sofas and their chatting dwindled to sleepy sighs.

Jordan awoke an hour later and the city of Wellington sprawled on the horizon. Letitia was on deck, steering the powerful boat, supervised by Nick. Jordan smiled at the nice picture the two of them made. It was kind of Nick to spend time connecting with the troubled teen.

"Letitia is going to talk to Russ about letting me join the Outreach team," Nick told her, as if it was something he'd always wanted to do. Jordan grinned, thinking if only he knew what he was getting himself into.

"Nick knows some people at the Marina," Letitia enthused, "and he's going to speak to them about teaching us water sports."

"I believe I said water safety," Nick cut in, reaching across her to nudge the wheel slightly.

Jordan had never seen him so relaxed and at ease. His teeth gleamed in his tanned face and his eyes shone when they looked at her. He was so breathtakingly handsome. She imagined drawing a frame around him, depicting with fine detail everything a man should look like, should be.

As she watched him smile and tease, and the young girl's shining face as she bantered with her new hero, something warm and heady washed over Jordan, through her. The cautionary walls she'd erected to protect herself melted and seeped away. Her heart began to beat, slow and strong, so strong she could feel it in her fingertips. A giddy feeling made her wobble on her seat and grab the side.

She loved him. It was as clear and shining and joyful as Christmas. She loved him and wanted him, and all the problems that would entail were as far away as the shoreline. Still there, still beckoning, but with a lower level of importance.

Nick said something to her and she was so distracted with her newfound knowledge, she had to ask him to repeat it. He reached out and ruffled her hair and she felt his hand there for long seconds after he'd taken it away, caressing, caring, branding her as his.

Once ashore, they reunited Letitia with her grateful parents and then Nick drove Jordan home. Her stomach growled as they entered her apartment, reminding her that the meager sandwich she'd had at lunch was many hours ago. "Would you like to stay for…"

"I thought you'd never ask," Nick growled, pushing her up against the wall in the passageway. Her bag hit the deck, her clothes were roughly pushed aside. He ravaged her mouth and she soared so high, so quickly as he took her against the wall. They didn't even make the bedroom.

Nick stayed the night, waking her early to make love once more before he had to go to the office. Jordan linked her arms around his neck as he kissed her goodbye. "Aren't you forgetting something?"

He smiled and leaned forward to sear her with another kiss.

"The sales agreement?" she laughed.

"Ah." He nodded. "I'll have my lawyer witness it."

"What are you going to do with it?" Jordan asked, leaning back on her pillows, looking like Aphrodite.

"I haven't decided yet," he told her. "Maybe I'll turn it into an exclusive art gallery and exhibit some starving but brilliant artist who's got a bunch of insecurities about her work."

Her eyes shone with amusement.

"And people will come from miles around," he continued, enjoying himself, "and she'll be famous the world over."

Jordan chuckled. "Except that no one will ever know because the gallery is so exclusive, no one can find it."

"Which will add greatly to her fame, in turn, making her forever grateful to me."

Nick found he liked this, waking with someone, sex, chatter and banter before getting on with the day. The prospect of making it a permanent arrangement entered his mind. It was a win-win, as far as he was concerned. He enjoyed her company, and the sex was beyond incredible.

"Did you get around to having plans drawn up for the refurbishment?"

"As a matter of fact, I did," she said, her eyes shining.

"Give me a look at them sometime."

Jordan kissed him fervently and asked if she'd see him Friday.

Nick groaned. "Friday is eons away. I have to go to Sydney on Wednesday for a meeting, but I'll be back late Thursday." He lifted a strand of her hair, ran it slowly through his fingers. "You'll be in court today, right?"

Jordan inhaled, her expression becoming cautious. "Nick…"

He knew what she was going to say: Don't let anyone know that they were together. Not that they'd articulated anything yet… "Don't worry," he reassured her, bending for one last taste of her lips. "We'll talk about it later."

He drove to his apartment, struggling to keep the smile off his face, an alien concept to his facial muscles, he was sure. This was a watershed weekend, one which had gone exactly to plan. She was crazy about him, he saw it in her face every time she looked at him. And that was just fine by Nick. Things were moving along smoothly and he was enjoying the ride.

He showered, changed and headed in to the office, looking forward to seeing her in court in an hour or so. He wondered if anyone would guess they'd spent the weekend together, if something would show in the way he looked at her.

"I'll be back after lunch—probably," Nick told Jasmine as he left for court. Adam and Randall had gone on ahead after the court clerk had called to confirm that Syrius was fit to attend.

Leaving the office building, he noticed an eye-catching pale blue limousine parked outside. He noticed it because he'd seen it before somewhere. The driver leaned against the car but straightened when he saw him and tapped on the back window, then gestured for Nick to approach. He did so, frowning.

The back window slid down. "Hello Nick," Elanor Lake said pleasantly. "May I have a few minutes of your time?"

After a moment's hesitation, Nick got into the limo and sat opposite her, his mind racing.

Jordan definitely got her looks from her mother. Soft golden hair clouded around Elanor's face. Her skin was creamy and smooth, her clothes elegant. She regarded him in a friendly, frank manner. The driver remained outside and Elanor pressed the window control closed.

"What can I do for you, Mrs. Lake?"

"It's Elanor," she said. "And I want you to stop seeing my daughter."

He saw from her demeanor that there was no point denying it. "I would gladly do almost anything you asked of me," he said sincerely, a slight inflection on the word you; his father's guilt ran deep. "But not that."

Her facial muscles tightened and she studied him at length. "This has gone further than I thought," she said finally.

Nick wondered if it was she monitoring her daughter's movements.

"I've always liked you, Nick. I've watched you grow, followed your career. You're well known for being straight. Responsible."

He inclined his head. Her approval of him could be

helpful in the bun fight that would ensue when Syrius found out.

Elanor sat back clasping her hands in her lap. "My husband has heart disease. It's quite serious. If he finds out about this—affair—it will possibly kill him. If it doesn't kill him straight off, then he will take a gun and shoot you."

Nick pretended to give it due consideration, allowing three heartbeats to go by. "I'll take my chances, but thank you for the warning."

"You're not listening. I believe you are an honorable man. Your mother was my best friend for many years. We resumed our friendship in secret a couple of years before she died."

Nick remembered then that's where he'd seen the limo. At the cemetery on the day of his mother's funeral. The windows were tinted and he couldn't identify the occupant. The car left before the end of the interment.

"Your mother was incredibly proud of you. She said you were honest and fair-minded. Very strong without the headstrong traits of your brother. She said you could always be relied upon to do exactly the right thing."

It seemed to Nick she enunciated every syllable with great care—*do exactly the right thing*. He continued watching her steadily, waiting for her to get to the point. His family owed her a hearing.

"Nick, I've watched my husband struggle over the years to try to modify his personality, and fail to do so. I've watched him have affairs and that's all right because I can't give him what he needs, and he always comes home to me. He treats me with the utmost care and allows me my dignity by being discreet. He loves me." Elanor leaned forward, watching his face intently. "But that love pales in comparison to what he feels for his daughter. Syrius loves Jordan more than his own life."

Nick grappled with some residual familial guilt that had unfairly passed down from his father. He and Jordan should never have started…it was self-indulgent and irresponsible. But it was too late now. "Elanor, I am sorry for what my father did to you. He is sorry for what he did to you. But it's unfair to expect Jordan and me to take the rap for past mistakes."

Her eyes were bright with sharp emotion. "I lost everything in that accident. My unborn son, only three weeks from birth. The use of my legs when my greatest passion—and my career—was dancing."

Nick flinched and swallowed to clear the ball of sympathy that had closed his throat.

Elanor saw it and her mouth thinned. "Syrius will never accept this relationship, do you understand?" She raised her hand, pointing at him. "Your father took his son. He would die rather than let a Thorne have his daughter."

Nick felt the blood drain from his face. He wanted to look away but a twisted respect forced him to keep eye contact.

Elanor wasn't finished. "I will lose everything. Again. Jordan will never be able to look at you without seeing the tragedy of what will confront her beloved father, who will be either dead or in prison. Your own father will probably cut you off."

He could only stare at her. For the first time, he began to truly understand the magnitude of the battle ahead.

"And all for a sordid turn between the sheets once a week. Something you could get from anyone."

Nick inhaled. He wasn't having that. "I care for her. I believe she cares for me." He knew she did.

A ghost of a smile softened her lips for a second. "Jordan falls in and out of love every other week."

He wouldn't dignify that with a response.

Now her eyes implored him. "I beg you, Nick, on your mother's love for me, do the right thing."

He knew his facial expression hadn't changed, outwardly resolute, but it was a different story inside. Emotions that he wasn't accustomed to slammed him, one after the other. Pity for the woman in front of him. Injustice that he and Jordan should pay the price for their fathers' sins. And anger that Elanor obviously had no intention of broaching the subject with her daughter. That meant it was up to him. If he agreed to her demands, if he agreed to finish it, he was the bad guy.

He couldn't give her what she wanted. Not yet, not without a fight. Hadn't his mother been on the mark? Want something you shouldn't. Take something you have no right to. He raised his chin. "I'll talk to Jordan. *We'll* decide."

He reached for the door handle but she laid her hand flat on his arm. When he looked back, the respectful demeanor of a minute ago had lapsed into ominous regret.

"Then you leave me no choice but to take this information to your father."

Nick settled back in the seat, rallying for another blow. Randall would hate it, there was no doubt about that. He needed to prepare the ground first.

"Nick," Elanor said quietly, "you've worked hard to get where you are, yet still your father stalls about naming you as his successor." She paused, building the tension. "You being involved with the daughter of his most bitter enemy would be a big strike against you, wouldn't it? He'd wonder about your loyalty."

Nick said nothing but silently agreed. Loyalty was a favorite catch phrase of Randall's.

"One strike against you in this situation is bad enough. Two might just tip the balance."

Nick frowned. What did she mean? A fatalistic sense of foreboding stabbed him at the sympathy in Elanor Lake's eyes.

"What's the other?"

"You're not his natural son, Nick," she said quietly. "You're not even legally adopted."

Eleven

Nick drove straight home after leaving Elanor's car and took his birth certificate from the safe. His mind soared with relief. She was lying. It was a bare-faced lie by a bitter woman intent on having her own way. Obviously Syrius didn't hold all the vindictive cards in his family.

But still, something inside him continued to niggle. He drove to his parents' house and asked the house-keeper where the family photos were stored. It was a standing family joke that if it moved, his mother photographed it. Nick spent hours poring through boxes and albums, searching out familial similarities. Nothing conclusive came of it. He was bigger, broader than his brother. His facial features were thicker than either of his parents, while Adam bore a striking resemblance to his mother. Coloring and eyes were similar enough to all members of the family to reassure him.

His scant relief receded when he opened a pack marked Pregnancy and flicked through tens of snaps of his mother during pregnancy but they were all dated 1979. Adam's year of birth, not his. Feverishly, Nick went through the rest of the box but was unable to find one picture of his mother pregnant in 1975.

He drove back to the office, told Jasmine he was not to be disturbed and sat there for the rest of the day, building up a good head of steam.

Had they treated him differently? He racked his brain for childhood memories. Nick was the eldest, mature beyond his years so he got lumbered with most of the chores and was expected to keep an eye on his younger brother. Elder kids always thought their younger siblings were spoiled and he was no exception. But one thing about Adam, he followed Nick around every-where, "helping" him, he'd say.

The bond was real between the brothers, but he wondered about his parents. They weren't the hands-on parents of modern times because they'd always put career first. Randall worked tirelessly building up his financial business while Melanie ran her dance studio six days a week. Public—or even private—displays of affection were rare.

He checked his watch for the umpteenth time. This rated as the longest day of his life. No matter how often he cautioned himself not to jump to conclusions, something told him Elanor had spoken the truth. Recent events backed it up. His mother leaving the share package to Adam, her *natural born son*. His father wanting Adam, his *natural born son*, to run the company.

The moment Randall returned from the court, Nick marched into his office, threw the birth certificate on his desk and demanded the truth. Randall insisted on knowing who he'd been talking to; when Nick told him, he blanched and did not deny it. And Nick faced the fact that up until now, his whole life had been a sham.

Two years after their marriage, the Thornes were told that they could never have children. Coming on the heels of the accident and Syrius's decree that banned Melanie from seeing his wife, Nick's mother fell into a state of deep depression. Randall, acutely aware of his business reputation, ensconced her in a luxury villa in one of Sydney's beach suburbs and commuted between Wellington and Sydney every other week.

Deeply depressed and lonely, his wife befriended a pregnant and unmarried housemaid. The next thing Randall knew, they had arranged an illegal adoption. Much money passed hands. Melanie even procured a forged birth certificate naming the Thornes as parents. Nearly a year after she'd left, Melanie returned to New Zealand with Nick in her arms. The couple maintained that he was their own miracle child. Four years later, against all odds, Melanie became pregnant with Adam.

"Did you know about this?" Nick asked Adam, who'd unwittingly walked into the tense confrontation.

"God's truth, I didn't," Adam assured him. "But it doesn't make a scrap of difference. You're my brother, Nick."

"Nor to me," his father said shakily. "Blood or not, you're my son."

"I want details," Nick declared. "Names, dates…"

"What's the point, Nick? We raised you as a Thorne, loved you from day one. Why rake it all up again?"

"Afraid you'll go to prison for fraud, not to mention buying a baby?" Nick looked at him scathingly, then immediately felt wretched. He softened his tone. "I'm going to Sydney tonight rather than Wednesday. I don't know when I'll be back. I need the address of the villa, her name, her lover—my father's—name, the dates she worked there…"

He wondered if his birth parents had ever contacted the Thornes again. Had they ever wanted to see him, or was it all about the money? Nick wondered what he was worth. "I see now why you want Adam to run the company, not me."

He heard Adam's sharp, indrawn breath, but his eyes were on his father's pale face.

"That's not true," Randall's voice implored him. "Not just Adam, not just you. Both of you."

Nick saw a world of fear in Randall's eyes. How long had he worried over this day?

Even so, he couldn't bring himself to say "Dad." Not yet.

"Nick, my feelings remain the same in regard to the company—and you." Adam lounged in his chair, seemingly relaxed but his expression was bleak, his face as pale as his father's.

Nick stood abruptly, knowing he had to get home and pack for the flight he'd booked earlier. "I'll be leaving for the airport in about two hours. Call me with those details."

"I'll come with you," Adam said quickly, rising.

Nick stopped and turned to face his brother.

Not his brother. Not even his legal adoptive brother… "This is something you can't help me with…"

"But…" Adam looked as stunned as Nick felt and it hit him a vicious blow. They were close, always had been. They even looked like each other. God's little joke… All these years, they'd believed in that blood bond, enjoyed each other's company, missed each other when they were apart. Would this revelation dent or change their relationship? How could it not?

Nick reached out and patted Adam awkwardly on the arm. "Thanks anyway, but I'd prefer to do this on my own."

Jordan left the courtroom on Monday, disconcerted about Nick's absence. When he didn't show up for the rest of the week, she began to worry. Which days had he said he'd be away? She'd been half asleep when he'd kissed her goodbye.

Calling his office was out and he didn't answer his cell phone. Not wanting to be labeled a nag, she decided against leaving a message but her unease grew with each passing day.

When he stood her up at the hotel on Friday, her

miserable confusion gave way to anger. Was he just playing with her? Surely she wasn't alone in thinking they'd forged new ground last weekend in the Sounds.

Heedless of being recognized, she inquired about the booking. "I'm sorry, the booking we have for Room 812 was cancelled on Monday," the receptionist said and looked at her with such pity that Jordan hurried out without another word, feeling quite ill.

Come to think of it, she'd felt unwell yesterday, too, but passed it off as nerves. A fleeting thought that she might be pregnant crossed her mind but she dismissed that. Nick always used protection, even though she was on the pill.

That day, she felt entitled to leave a message on his voicemail and his house phone, which also went unanswered. And even though she felt nauseous and lonely, she forced herself to go out that night to a film premiere with two friends. They bumped into Jason Cook and went clubbing. When Nick didn't call over the rest of the weekend, even after she'd left several more messages, she went out both nights and made sure she was photographed.

The trial entered its expected last week, but still Nick didn't show and her phone remained silent. Oh, why had she allowed herself to hope, to believe that she was enough for him? She would have been happy, she *was* happy knowing it was just sex, until he made her fall in love with him.

Forget him! She called Jason and a few of the party hounds she used to spend time with. It was easy to slip right back into party mode, like the Jordan of old. Club openings, premieres, she attended every glitzy occasion she could think of to court the press. Even the tummy bug that lingered didn't stop her, although she was unable to stomach alcohol. Nick Thorne had blown it, she thought angrily. No one rejected Jordan Lake! She intended to make him so jealous he'd come crawling and then, she'd kick him aside like a dog.

Only he didn't come crawling. Jordan played at being the life of the party because she dreaded going to bed. The only way she could contain the pain slicing her up inside was to curl into a ball, rocking and hugging herself hard enough to bruise her flesh. In this bed, he had made love to her, had kissed her goodbye for the last time. Unshed tears dogged her day and night, making her eyes and throat ache. What was so wrong with her that he didn't want her anymore?

One night in a crowded club, someone tapped her on the shoulder and she turned to find Adam Thorne smiling down at her.

"Are you going to have me thrown out of here as well?" he asked jovially.

Jordan responded to his friendly manner like a lifeline. They'd never had an official introduction so they remedied that now. Her friends raised their brows and whispered about how hot he was. Adam was considered one of the most eligible bachelors in the city. But she could see little of Nick in his face. There was no magic there.

She longed to ask about him but knew the hurt was

too close. Her heart may just break and bleed all over the floor. No one must see how empty and sad and hurt she was.

Adam stood behind her chair, bending his head to hear over the music. They chatted for some time about the case and their impossible fathers. "You know, I told Nick the best way to end this stupid feud is to hook up with you."

The knife in her heart twisted painfully but she managed to keep some semblance of a smile, she hoped. "Really? When?"

"When the trial started." Adam sent a huge smile of welcome to a pretty woman who'd just entered the club. Jordan recognized her as Nick's secretary.

"Nick wants to run Thorne's," Adam said distractedly. "He can't do that while the old man is around, and the old man is so busy chasing your old man around a courtroom, he won't retire."

"And what did Nick say?" she asked faintly, chewing on the straw of her drink.

Adam straightened, still looking at the woman. "Oh, Nick's way too clever to take my advice. It was nice meeting you at last, Jordan Lake. See you in court." He paused and winked at her. "I've always wanted to say that."

Jordan sat for at least a minute with the same stupid, dazed smile on her mouth, trying to make sense of it. He had a plan? A sick dread blanketed down over the misery of unrequited love in her heart.

Was it right from the start? she thought dazedly—no, Adam had said the start of the trial. That was about the time things changed between them. He'd started bringing gifts and acting jealous.

She tried to breathe but the ache inside constricted her chest. Dear God, he'd planned it all along. He didn't want her. This wasn't about them. It was a cold, calculated plan to get her to fall in love with him and realize his ambitions.

The reality twisted the knife some more, causing bile to rush to her throat. She rushed to the bathroom where she was violently sick. Someone helped her out of the club and into a cab. And the tabloids faithfully reported her incapacity the next day.

"You're certainly burning the candle at both ends, dear," her mother commented. "What on earth were you drinking?"

"I hadn't had anything," Jordan said defensively. Her mother had a knack of drawing her secrets to the fore. Her broken heart was one secret she wouldn't discuss, not with her mother or anyone else. She couldn't bear the humiliation. "I have a bug, that's all."

By day, she sat in court, staring stiffly ahead, acutely aware of the empty space across the aisle. After her fifth consecutive night out, she was exhausted and low as she could ever remember feeling. The lack of sleep and this interminable tummy bug had her head spinning, so on Wednesday night, she bought a home pregnancy test. It was just a precaution. She was ninety-nine percent certain she wasn't pregnant; surely she'd feel something—a bond, a connection—instead of just miserable and confused and god-awful sick.

The digital display on the stick flashed *Pregnant.*

No, no, no. This couldn't be happening.

When was her last period? Things had been so up in the air lately. Working bees, nosy newspapers, charity balls. Nick. Taking a deep breath, churning up with nerves, she took the second stick from the box.

She was late to court on Thursday. Her heels seemed inordinately loud on the wooden floor as she entered. Heads turned in the gallery and the judge gave her a baleful look. "Sorry," she whispered loudly.

And then she saw. He turned his head and looked straight at her, his expression cold. Scathing.

Jordan sat shakily, absorbing the rush of elation that always came with seeing his face. The emptiness inside her began to fill...but then his icy expression filtered through her joy.

Her stomach churned. What gave him the right to look at her like that? It was she who should feel aggrieved. He'd used and discarded her without so much as a word.

You have to tell him.

"Not yet," she whispered. Her mother turned and looked at her, eyes full of concern. Jordan could only shake her head mutely.

Not yet. Home pregnancy tests were not foolproof. She would say nothing until she had seen a doctor. Which doctor? She couldn't rely on the discretion of the Elpis Clinic doctors—they were all volunteers.

He'd think she'd trapped him. Worse, he'd question

whether he was the father. So many morbid thoughts surged through her brain, even as common sense told her Nick was a decent, responsible man. He'd do the right thing by her.

It was the longest morning of her life. She made it until lunchtime, then bolted for the bathroom, throwing up for the third time that week.

When she came out, Nick was about to descend the steps outside, alone. Jordan felt like death but she couldn't cope with the misery any longer. Forcing herself to stop shaking, she filled her heart with steely determination.

He'd shoved his hands in his pockets and his head was bowed. For a brief moment, as she approached, she thought he looked unhappy. But then all the tortured hours of the last week or so swamped her. He'd made her feel a failure as a woman, a lover, a friend. She wasn't about to let him off scot free. She strode up behind him, grasping his arm firmly. "I want to talk to you."

As he swung around to face her, just for a second, she saw something so uplifting, so eager in his face, as if he was glad to see her. But then the shutters came down like the night. His cold, closed expression slayed her.

This wasn't the man she knew—*thought* she knew. This was someone else entirely. She almost quailed before him and if she hadn't just lost her breakfast, that would have been a real possibility.

Nick glanced around quickly. "This isn't the time or…"

"Well, if you'd returned my calls…" Jordan felt like she was swimming in treacle. But then he grasped her arm and pulled her around the side of the building, out of sight of the trickle of people emerging from the court.

"I'm surprised you could drag yourself out of bed this morning—whose bed was it today? Do you even remember?"

Oh, that was a slap in the face. Okay, she had played the party girl this week but that was down to him.

She pried her arm out of his grasp. "What *is* it with you?" she demanded. "All over me one minute, then nothing?" Her voice rose high and shrill and she sucked in a furious breath. She didn't know him. His tight, hard face mocked her. A nasty, bilious taste rose from her chest, burning her throat.

She swayed, fear flooding her. Fear that she'd throw up right here. Fear that the next words said would be their final words ever. "I thought we had—" her voice cracked and broke "—something special."

His expression did not change. She hadn't reached him, only given him another chance to kick her. A hard little knot of anger formed. That was a mistake she wouldn't make again.

"Looks like you've been enjoying a lot of something special with a lot of men," he muttered, not looking at her as if the sight of her made him sick. "How's *Jason?*"

"Jason's just fine," she retorted. Apart from a dose of frustration, since she'd spurned his advances all week. Nick had no reason to be jealous.

"How many men, Jordan?" he asked in a deadly low voice. "How many does it take to satisfy you?"

This was too much. She had done nothing wrong!

She was the one who'd been wronged. "You have no right to ask me that," she told him angrily. "Not when it was all a lie. You used me. It was all about the job, wasn't it? Getting a promotion?"

Nick flinched and she saw she'd hit the mark. She wanted to howl with rage. "You wanted the feud finished and thought being with me would do it. All you had to do was lay on the charm and you knew I'd take it seriously, poor, gullible fool I am."

He recovered fast. "Let me tell you something, no one takes you seriously, Jordan Lake. You're just a spoiled little rich girl who dabbles in charity work with about as much feeling as you dabble in men."

Jordan saw red, buckets of it. Her gut churned with injustice. The hurt and anger rolled through her with impetus. She straightened her spine and fixed him with as imperious a look as she could muster. "Well, you better start taking me seriously, since I'm carrying your baby!"

Nick jerked back as if she'd slapped him. The blood drained from his face so quickly, a tangible dragging that left him lightheaded. He thought he heard his stomach gurgle.

Pregnant? His whole world crashed around him. On top of the week he'd just endured, this was too much. He stared at her face, her deathly pale face. Pregnant? His lips moved soundlessly, shaping the word.

"You can't be," he managed in a strangled whisper. "I always protected you."

He had. Who knew about Jason Cook? "You're on the Pill."

She stared back, eyes wide open and shocked, her lips firmly pressed together.

Nick took a step back, fighting for control. So many revelations, so many life-altering shocks, one on top of the other. But this...this was the last thing he expected.

Jordan was never far from his mind over the ten days he'd been away but between business, meeting his mother and trying to ascertain his father's whereabouts, he couldn't bring himself to call her. He was picking through an emotional minefield. With Elanor's demands that he finish it still ringing in his ears, his pedigree—or lack of— added another dimension, another burden to bear. These were things best said in person, not over the phone.

But he didn't expect to have to read about her in the newspapers and woman's magazines. Headlines leapt out at him, everywhere he went, at his mother's house, walking past bookstores in Sydney's business district, the plane on the way home. A quick trip to the Internet got him hundreds of hits on Jordan Lake's antics since he'd been away. Everyone seemed very excited about her reconciliation with Jason Cook, although apparently she wasn't limiting herself and had been seen with others. Being snapped drunk and sick with alcohol poisoning just capped it all off perfectly. She was weak, he realized, weak and self-indulgent. Not what he needed right now.

As far as Nick was concerned, Elanor Lake had done him a huge favor.

Now she stood in front of him, pale and weary from her hectic social life, telling him she was pregnant. To him?

Glancing around quickly—the ramifications if this little tidbit got out did not bear thinking about—he swung back to her, glowering.

"I want the truth right now," he gritted. "Are you pregnant—by me—or not?"

A sheen of perspiration glowed on her upper lip, lips that had drained of color. Her normally vibrant skin looked thin as tissue, but Nick clamped down on a spurt of unwelcome worry. Get the truth—and the proof—and decide what to do about it then.

She blinked quickly, opened her mouth. God help him, she looked as shocked as he felt. Even her anger would be better than this frozen-in-the-headlights look. "Well, you can't blame me for asking," he said roughly.

Her trembling mouth firmed. "You stood me up, you bastard. Not so much as a phone call. Just how long did you expect me to sit around waiting?"

The bleak wind of betrayal went through him, spreading its poison. "Poor little Jordan," he said wearily, feeling like he'd gone ten rounds with Mike Tyson. "You've just got to be the center of attention, haven't you?"

She backed off, swallowing, her eyes sliding all the way to his shoes. Her head was down, and for the first time, he noticed that her hair, her beautiful golden hair, looked lank and lifeless. A hank of it fell forward over her face. And then she looked up at him, and he reeled at the disappointment in her eyes.

"You're just like everyone else, aren't you?" Her voice held an element of surprise.

Nick wanted to rage, to put his hands on her and shake the disappointment out of her. But somehow he couldn't do anything other than glower down at this woman, this addiction he had, this spoiled, self-indulgent woman who'd filled a hole inside of him that he hadn't even known was there.

Pregnant! How ironic. Someone had gotten pregnant thirty-four years ago, but had decided money was more important than raising a child. Illegitimate, disenfranchised—he wasn't even adopted.

"Nick!" Adam called from the top of the steps. "The judge is coming back."

The verdict was expected today. Jordan hadn't even glanced up when Adam had spoken. Nick exhaled loudly. "I can't deal with this right now."

She raised her head slowly, met his eyes. He didn't want to read what was in hers.

"You don't have to *deal* with anything," she said curtly, then spun on her heel and walked away.

Nick's head rolled back and he looked skyward, feeling the anger ebb away. Now he just ached with wretched need and disappointment. She was like a drug to him, and despite everything, the withdrawal symptoms were powerful. But a drug was a drug. It pulled you down and sucked you dry. You had to kick it to survive.

Twelve

The judge gave his decision, awarding damages of five hundred thousand dollars to Randall Thorne. Everyone agreed it was a predictable outcome. Nick declined the celebratory drinks mooted and returned to the office, aware of Randall staring sadly after him.

He let Jasmine go early and poured himself a Scotch, trying to obliterate the memory of Jordan's face, twisted with anger and fear and—disappointment. In him.

Nick hated disappointing anybody. But Jordan— Jordan with the big blue eyes that reached in and touched him, connected with him on some level that no one else ever had. No matter how many times he told himself it was just an overpowering sexual attraction, he knew deep down it was real.

Having his baby…

Nick had decided weeks ago to go after her, forge a future with her to force an end to their father's feud. But this…this was definitely not what he envisaged. Not when he was only just getting his head around being illegitimate himself.

Did he believe her? Yes. She might cheat, she might make the wrong choices sometimes—Nick scowled, wanting to smash Jason Cook's face—but if she said the baby was his, it was his. She was too good a person to let him take the rap for someone else.

The Scotch slid down his throat smoothly. He listened to the sounds of the office packing up, the noises of the city down below. It rarely happened that Nick searched for answers in the bottom of a bottle. The foundations of his life had been swept away, but he was who he was. He would do the right thing by Jordan.

After all, that's what he'd wanted, eventually. Did it matter that the schedule had changed? Feud or no feud, his baby would not be born illegitimate, like him.

Randall knocked and poked his head around the door. "Son, we need to talk. There are things I should have said a long time ago."

Nick nodded toward the bottle and glasses. They hadn't spoken about their situation since his return from Australia. Now was as good a time as any.

"Nicky." His father brought his drink to the desk and sat, looking very ill at ease. Nick knew talking from the heart wasn't the old man's strong point; it never had been.

"If I've made you feel less important to me than

Adam, then I'm very sorry. It was unwittingly done. You mean just as much to me—did to your mother, too. I couldn't be more proud of you."

"I know that," Nick said gravely. "Which is why you'll cooperate when I get my lawyer to apply for a new birth certificate showing my birth parents' names." He watched Randall's cheeks hollow. "Did you know that I cannot be legally adopted in this country after the age of twenty?"

"I didn't know that."

"I doubt there will be consequences, after all this time," Nick continued, pursing his lips.

"I'll take the damn consequences," Randall interjected. "And while we're crossing the T's and dotting the i's, I'll make a new will naming you as an elected beneficiary, or whatever they want to call it."

Nick settled back in his chair.

"It's the least I can do," his father finished bleakly.

Nick studied the older man's face. It was time to press his case, once and for all. Perhaps he'd lose, perhaps he had underestimated Randall's feelings for him, but at least he'd go out trying. "It's taken me a while to figure out why you're reluctant to name me as managing director but I think I'm getting there."

His father started to interrupt but Nick stopped him. "You're afraid of being left alone. Mom's gone. Adam's in London. With this illegal adoption…hanging over your head all these years…so many years building a business that you want to live on after you're gone."

He sipped his Scotch, his gaze steady. "I may not be

your blood, Randall but I'm in this for the long haul. You've taught me—us—well. You need to have faith that you've done your job. Have I ever let you down?"

Randall shook his head at the quick question, subdued. "You never have."

"I won't leave you," Nick said firmly. "Nor will Adam. That's a promise. It's time you stopped worrying about this."

Randall was old school, brought up to keep his emotions carefully hidden. But Nick saw the love and support—for him—on his father's aged face and knew he was on the mark. "I may not be your blood, Randall," he repeated, "but I'm your best—no, I'm your *only*— option to take this place, keeping all your values and integrity intact, and grow it to pass on to my kids one day."

The old man's eyes gleamed and he suddenly found something very interesting in the bottom of his glass.

"And you'll be around to see it," Nick finished.

Randall sat for a minute, swallowing several times, his aged throat bobbing. Then he slowly got to his feet and came around to Nick's side of the desk. "Nick. Son." He extended his hand. Nick rose and they clasped hands. "I couldn't bear to lose you," his father mumbled, clapping him hard on the back in a semblance of an embrace.

Nick thought that might be the only time in his life his father had hugged him and he knew playing hardball and declaring his loyalty had been the right thing to do.

"Right, then," Randall huffed, drawing back, patting pockets, buttoning his jacket and generally doing a good impression of businesslike busyness. "You'd better start packing in here in preparation for your move to the corner office." He stepped back and raised his glass. "I'll announce it at the birthday party next week. Get yourself a new suit and bring a date."

Nick nodded. A date…since it was a day for revelations, he could do better than that, couldn't he? "Sit down, Dad. I have something else to say."

Jordan sat on the couch, leaning on Elanor's shoulder. "Do you think he'll be all right?"

Elanor nodded. "He'll appeal, just to be bloody-minded, but deep down he knew he'd lose. Even the lawyers warned him this was the likely outcome." She slipped her hand through her daughter's arm. "I'm more worried about you, rushing off like that."

Jordan heaved a heavy sigh. "I'm sorry. I just felt so ill." She hadn't been able to face going back into the courtroom after Nick's cold, hard put-down. His words his face—her throat closed and she was overwhelmed at last by the tears that had backed up for days, threatening to choke her.

She threw herself into her mother's lap and sobbed out the whole story, while Elanor stroked her hair and murmured comforting platitudes. Then, with typical pragmatism, she phoned her specialist and got Jordan an appointment immediately. "Home pregnancy kits aren't always accurate. We have to be sure."

Jordan washed her face and helped her mother into the car.

"Do you love him?" Elanor asked quietly.

That started a fresh round of crying. "With all my heart."

Mopping her face with tissues, she heard her mother sigh, and looked up. Elanor's yes were very troubled. "Oh, Jordan."

"I know. I'm spoiled and selfish, just like he said. He's the son of Dad's worst enemy, but did I let that stop me?" She shook her head miserably.

"Darling, it's not that. We can't always control these things." She took Jordan's hand. "I have a confession to make. I warned Nick off last week, insisted he stop seeing you."

Jordan's head jerked up. "How did you…?"

"I had you investigated," her mother said quietly.

Speechless, Jordan could only stare, wondering if she'd heard correctly.

"I'm sorry. Your social life until a few months ago was well documented. At least I had an idea of what was going on. But there has been no one for months, nearly a year. I just wanted to make sure you were all right. And when I found out who it was, I tried to scare him off."

"I can't believe you'd…" Jordan reeled with the revelation that her kind, sweet mother would go to these lengths. That sounded like something Syrius might do, but…another thought twisted through her over-loaded brain. "What—what did he say? Nick?"

Her mother bit her lip. "That he cared for you."

That should have elated her. It didn't. After the altercation earlier, it only intensified the ache.

"I didn't realize the extent of your feelings," Elanor

continued. "With the court case going on, your father would have exploded if he'd found out. But if I'd known how you felt about him, I would never have spoken to him…told him…" Her voice trailed off.

"Told him what?"

Her mother hesitated. "That's better coming from him. You need to talk to him."

"Except he doesn't want anything to do with me," Jordan said, sniffing. "Apart from your interference, I've spent the last week childishly trying to make him jealous. He thinks I'm sleeping with every man and his dog."

"I'm sure once he calms down and gets over the shock, he won't believe that."

The car turned into the consultant's car park. Jordan took out her compact and checked her face. "You sound almost hopeful." She grimaced at her red, swollen eyes and blotchy cheeks. If she was seen going into a private ob-gyn clinic looking like this, the press would have a field day. She tied her hair back hurriedly and slid her sunglasses on. "But the fact remains that Dad will never accept it."

"Let me deal with Syrius," her mother said grimly.

As they waited to be seen, Jordan tried to make sense of it all. If Nick had refused her mother's demands, what had happened between then and now, when he could barely look at her without disgust?

She had happened. Hurt by his silence, she had lived up to his expectations of her, as she so often did. What had he said? That she always had to be the center of attention.

The consultant took a blood test, which their on-site

lab rushed through. Less than two hours later, they returned to the car. Exhausted after the stress of the day—and of the last week or so—Jordan leaned back in the seat and turned her tear-streaked face to her mother. "Oh, Mom, it just hurts so much."

Elanor stroked Jordan's hair and wiped away her tears, her own eyes glistening.

"Can I stay with you tonight?" Jordan felt so helpless, so out of control. She needed the comfort of her old room, familiar surroundings, the arms and love and sympathy only a mother could provide.

"Of course you can," her mother murmured. "For as long as you like."

Nick tossed and turned all night, despite the whiskey sedative that should have ensured sleep. What was the matter with him? He'd achieved his goal. He would be named as the managing director of Thorne Enterprises the following week. He'd made peace with his father over his parentage and gotten to know his mother a little. Surely he had everything he wanted.

Except…the woman carrying his baby thought he wanted nothing to do with her. The pain in her eyes as he'd heaped insults and scorn upon her haunted him. He tried to justify his behavior by remembering the publicity of her partying up with her new/old lover. And she hadn't denied it—not that he'd given her much of a chance.

He should have called her; he knew that now. With her insecurities and mystifying low self-esteem, his lack of communication must have hurt. She wasn't responsible for what his personal life had served up to him. All she knew was that he'd stayed away.

The sunrise began to streak the sky with gold. Nick gave up on sleep, pulled on some track pants and sat on the step of his large, modern town house, cradling a mug of black coffee. Looking out over the easy-care garden, across the busy road that ran alongside the bay, he suddenly wondered if this house would be suitable for a child. Built on three levels, not fenced in—Lord, it was a death trap!

A baby. He allowed his mind to process the word, but found he couldn't assimilate it quite yet, couldn't conjure up a picture in his mind. But Jordan pregnant— now that was easier. She would make a beautiful mother-to-be. His mind wandered back to waking snuggled up behind her on the boat, and then he imagined his arms around her swelling middle, feeling the baby move, sharing the appointments, buying…whatever prospective parents bought in preparation for the event.

A ripple of exhilaration swept him from head to toe, and he threw his head back at the lightening sky. A baby. A chance to right the wrongs of the past. To stamp his identify on another human and show him or her that they were precious, wanted, loved.

Suddenly he could hardly wait to start sharing the experience. He had to wait, thought, since it was only five-thirty. He dragged on a T-shirt and some trainers and set off for a run along the stony beach, needing physical exertion to curb his growing elation at the thought of becoming a father.

And what of Jordan herself? He'd changed their intense and forbidden affair into another step on the ladder of his ambition. Technically, now that he had what he wanted, she was surplus to requirements. Pounding along the long stretch of beach, sweat dripping into his eyes, he asked himself the question: *if* he hadn't gone away and *if* she hadn't fallen pregnant and *if* she hadn't taken up with her former lover, would they have continued their affair, even after he'd been made managing director?

Yes. They would have. Other than their fathers' prejudices, he and Jordan were great together. The time, effort and resources she put into trying to make a difference suggested she would work hard to support his career and make their marriage and family succeed. He could help her grow in confidence and develop her foundation. Even now, as his lungs screamed, the incredible sexual pull that they shared had him wanting her more than his next breath. She was fun, kind and sexy. He felt comfortable with her and yet fiercely passionate about her.

And insanely jealous…. The storm clouds gathered in his mind as he turned for home, his steps accelerating. Nick would fight to the death to keep her. No one, neither Jason Cook nor her sanctimonious father, would keep him away from the woman he loved.

Nick rang the doorbell at the Lake mansion, filled with grim determination. Walking into the lion's den on the day after the verdict was not the most sensible thing he'd ever done, but he'd had no luck tracking Jordan at her apartment.

The Lake's housekeeper opened the door just as Elanor wheeled herself into the impressive entrance. "Thank you, Helen," she said, then dismissed the housekeeper, keeping her eyes on Nick. It may have been the early hour, but she looked strained, as if she hadn't slept.

Nick girded himself for battle. "Is she here?"

"She's upstairs. Nick…"

He hesitated, awash with relief. If she were here, her mother must know about the pregnancy. "What about Syrius? I'll need to talk to him."

"He left early to catch up now that the case is over."

Nick gave a brief nod and turned his eyes on the stairs. "Which room?"

"Second on the right. Nick…"

He paused, his jaw set with impatience.

Elanor sighed heavily, her face lined with sadness. "She's—fragile right now. Go easy on her."

Thirteen

Nick's eyes narrowed with concern. What was that supposed to mean? Morning sickness or something more sinister? He remembered her words in the car—Jordan falls in and out of love very other week. What if Elanor was trying to tell him that her daughter was in love with someone else or, worse, pregnant to someone else?

Elanor fidgeted under his gaze.

Nick needed to get those answers from Jordan herself, no one else. He knew her. She wouldn't lie about him being the father of the baby. He'd do whatever he had to, but he wasn't going to allow her to throw her life, her talent, her goodness away on a loser like Jason Cook.

He snapped off a brief nod and headed for the stairs.

As he reached the top, aware of Elanor's anxious eyes following his every step, a door opened and Jordan appeared in the hallway. They both stopped dead, staring. She wore a bright orange floral robe tied at the waist. She seemed to have lost weight. The robe clung to her as she stood, the sharp angle of her hip clearly showing through the flimsy fabric. Her hair was loose and brushed behind her ears.

She looked done in. Her eyes were pink and puffy, her lips paler than lilac. Nick stroke forward, filled with an irrational worry that she might fall if he didn't catch her, hold her up. "What is it? Are you sick?"

Her eyes widened as he approached, and she opened her mouth, but nothing came out. He reached out and ran his hand down her arm, needing to touch her, to make sure she wouldn't disappear into thin air.

Jordan shrank away, a tiny shift back that sliced at him. "What do you want, Nick? If my father…"

He shook his head, stung by her disapproving tone. "I went to your place," he began curtly.

"And naturally you assumed I was with someone else." Her surprise had cooled into sullen weariness.

"Whatever happened in the past week," Nick ground out, "we have to put it behind us."

Jordan swallowed and looked away. He imagined it was guilt making her chew her bottom lip, but then reminded himself of his purpose. The baby came first. Whatever mistakes she'd made—they'd both made— they could work on forgiving each other after he had an assurance from her that they had a future together. "I'm not blaming you, but I won't let you throw your life away on that loser."

She blinked. "You won't let me…who?"

"Jason!" he snarled, his jealousy perilously close to the surface. "Your ex—and soon-to-be ex again."

She huffed out a weary breath, shaking her head slightly. "You really believe I've been sleeping around?"

Yes. No. Hell, all he wanted was her denial.

"Haven't you noticed," she said with exaggerated patience, "that the papers don't care about true or false? If I trip over, it's because I'm drunk or on drugs. If I say hello to someone on the street, I'm engaged."

"You said yesterday—you intimated…"

"Oh, Nick." She sighed. "Can't you recognize when a woman is in love with you?"

Nick stared at her, the wind knocked completely out of his sails. She loved him. There was no one else.

Jordan stood in front of him, rocking on her heels a little. But at least some of the color was returning to her cheeks. She was still the most beautiful woman he had ever seen. Relief and elation threatened to overwhelm him.

"I didn't deny your accusations," she continued, "because you hurt me so much. You just disappeared off the face of the earth. I didn't know what I'd done. And when you looked at me like that yesterday…" Her voice broke. "Why, Nick? Why did you brush me off like I was something on your shoe?"

Nick closed his eyes against the pain darkening hers. Unfamiliar emotions slammed him. Elation that she loved him, relief that she wanted no one else, guilt for putting that pain on her lovely face. Moving purely on instinct, he reached out and took both her hands in his. "Didn't your mother tell you what was going on?"

Her hands lay limply in his. "She told me she warned you off. And that she'd had me investigated." Her voice was listless, as if declaring her love had drained her of energy.

She really looked done in. Nick pointed his chin at the door behind her. "Can we sit down?"

Jordan led him into a large, feminine bedroom. The colors were peach and sage green. The windows overlooked the rhododendron garden that the Lake mansion was quite famous for. His eyes darted to the sports and dancing trophies lining one massive bookcase, and to a clutch of photos of her at a young age, wearing ballet costumes or a net-ball skirt or a school uniform. He wanted to inspect them more closely, but she had sunk down onto an unmade queen-sized bed. As he joined her, she grabbed a pillow, hugging it to her stomach.

"I was away," he began, wary of implicating her mother in this part of it.

"Sydney." She nodded.

"I found out I wasn't Randall's son, or my mother's. I was—purchased."

Nick still couldn't believe it himself. He knew Randall and Melanie loved him, as did Adam. As for his birth mother, he'd made a start, and was grateful she'd given him up to the best possible family.

But he needed to be with Jordan. He needed her love

to make him whole. She was home to him in a way he'd never felt before.

He felt the pressure of her hand on his shoulder, warming him, as welcome as the comfort, acceptance and empathy that showed in her eyes.

"I spent ten days in Australia, tracking my birth parents. I thought of you—often—but it was just so complicated. I didn't want to get into it on the phone."

"Did you find them?" she asked after a few seconds.

"My mother, yes. Not my father, though I've got some leads I'll probably check out."

"Did you like her?"

He nodded. "She's nice, has her own family. She'd like to keep in touch." At least he'd gotten one thing clear in his mind. "She may have given birth to me but Melanie was my mother."

Jordan's hand slid off his shoulder. He missed it immediately.

"How did Randall take all this?"

"I think he's been expecting it—dreading it—for years. It's probably a relief."

Jordan looked down at her feet, swallowing. "That's huge, Nick. I wish you would have told me."

He should have, he knew that now. Maybe he was afraid that with all the barriers to them being together, his illegitimacy might be the last straw. Jordan wasn't the only one capable of holding things back.

"Nick, I need to know if you planned this whole thing so you could get a promotion."

He'd wondered when she'd get around to this. "We

met, fell into bed, kept meeting. Jordan, I lived for our Fridays. When the case started, Adam made a lighthearted suggestion that a union between us might persuade our fathers to cool it, stop with the fighting and the legal battles. That comment fell on fertile ground because I was already halfway there. It wasn't exactly a hardship," he said earnestly, taking her hands in his. "We're good together. Everything that grew out of that was real."

Her thoughtful expression gave no clue as to whether she believed him.

"Anyway, it's a moot point now. Dad's going to announce it next week. You're looking at the new managing director of Thorne Enterprises."

She smiled faintly, "Congrats."

Nick hadn't expected much enthusiasm under the circumstances, but still, he squeezed her fingers and ducked his head to peer into her eyes quizzically. "Jordan, I'm so sorry about yesterday, and the lack of communication. I never meant to hurt you."

She looked down at their joined hands. "I can't remember ever feeling so—" her shoulders rose and fell "—low."

"Hormones, I suppose," he said, thinking of the pregnancy. "This puts everything in a new light. Jordan," he said, reaching out to smooth a rogue strand of hair behind her ears. "I want our baby to be born legitimate, not like me. I want us to make a good home for him or her, a great family home…why are you crying?"

Tears began to slide down her face, and his heart did an ominous slide in his chest.

"I should never have said anything," she blurted. "Not until I was sure, but I've been sick, and the home test was positive—twice—and you got me so riled..." She tugged her hands away from his and covered her face.

He sat there stupidly, wondering what she meant, helpless in the face of her distress.

"I'm not pregnant, Nick," she said sadly from behind her hands. "I never was."

Jordan couldn't look at him, but felt his eyes on her. The sadness pressed down, making her neck ache. "Mom took me to a specialist yesterday for a blood test, and it came back negative." A shuddering sigh caught her unawares and she pressed the pillow into her stomach. "I'm supposed to go back in a couple of days for anther test, but I probably won't bother since I got my period in the night."

"But you were sick."

She shrugged, still not looking at him. "Nerves. Stress. A bug..."

They sat there for a minute in silence. She didn't want to see his relief. In reality, she should be relieved herself, having no desire to raise a baby on her own. But all she felt was a dragging grief, as if someone close had died and nothing would ever be the same again.

Nick cleared his throat. "No baby," he said, as if he still couldn't believe it. She braved a look at his face. Incredibly, he looked dazed and terribly disappointed.

Disappointed? He was off the hook. "You must be relieved."

She immediately wished the words back when he swallowed and looked away. "Relieved?" His eyes tracked slowly around each wall of the big room, an excruciatingly slow inspection, before finally coming full circle to her face again. "I don't know," he said slowly. "It's amazing how quickly I got used to the idea, even embraced the idea, of having a baby with you."

That was unexpected, although finding out recently that he wasn't who he thought he was probably had something to do with it. While she mulled that over, Nick reached out and lifted her chin, his eyes full of concern.

"How do you feel about it?"

"Sad," she whispered. She'd already told him she loved him. She didn't have to hide anything now. "It was something of you, and the most worthwhile and important part of me." She shrugged again. "So I thought, for a few hours, anyway."

Nick slid his hands up her arms and around her back to draw her close. It was a relief to hide her face in his chest, to rest against all that clean warmth and solid support. She closed her eyes.

"There'll be other babies," Nick muttered into her hair. "It doesn't change how I feel about you."

She smiled gently, remembering. "Your luxury." But she knew she couldn't go back to what they were. Everything had changed. She wanted to be worth something now. "Our Fridays are in the past," she said firmly, as if to convince herself. Would she ever feel the same burning need for anyone else? Perhaps companionship and common goals might be a safer gamble next time.

"I agree." His arms tightened around her. "But I still want to marry you."

Jordan snuggled in close, mentally saying goodbye to their Friday afternoons. Nick's words took an age to filter into her woolly brain. Lack of sleep, of food, of anything resembling sunshine since their weekend away on the boat had withered her comprehension.

Had he just said he wanted to marry her?

She leaned back a little, squinting over the crisp collar and blue silk tie, past the strong, square chin and into his piercing eyes. Her heart gave a healthy kick.

No trace of amusement sullied Nick's serious contemplation of her. Instead, he reached down and curled his fingers around her hand, squeezing gently. "I love you, Jordan, and I still want to marry you, baby or not."

Her eyes filled, and a lump the size of Gibraltar invaded her throat. She shook her head impatiently. Why cry when she'd just heard the words she wanted to hear more than anything in the world? When she lay encircled in the arms of the man she loved more than anything in the world? When the sincerity and love shone from his eyes, soothing the hurt of the past few days, giving her hope for the future? "Really?" she asked, aware of how inadequate the question was. But her mind hadn't yet cleared for takeoff.

Nick laced their fingers together and raised her hand to his mouth. "Really," he murmured. "I *really* love you, Jordan."

She shivered—delayed reaction. She could listen to those words all day.

"It was inevitable," he continued, "once I got to know you, saw how hard you tried, how generous and giving you were. So sexy, you should be illegal." He kissed her knuckles one by one. "You accepted me, although I gave you little enough. And I hate that it took me so long, and all this upset, to realize how I feel."

A bit, fat tear escaped and slid slowly down her cheek. "Oh, Nick, I love you so much, it hurts."

"Perhaps this will ease your pain." He wrapped her up in his arms and bent his head to kiss her. At the first touch of his lips on hers, she tensed, waiting for the irresistible thrill that never failed to suck the breath from her lungs and sent her heart galloping. But this was a healing kiss, a kiss to say sorry, a tender, nourishing lifeline that she never wanted to let go of. She relaxed into contentment, trying to burrow closer, loving his clean, warm scent and the strength of his arms around her.

"There is still," he told her a minute later, when he'd stopped kissing her into next week, "the matter of how your father is going to take this."

She blinked slowly, still dazed by that kiss. "Mom likes you. She's an amazing woman, my mother." Jordan couldn't quite believe Elanor had spied on her. "I'm only starting to realize *how* amazing—and exactly who wears the pants around here." She smiled up into Nick's eyes, feeling quite light-headed with happiness. Her stomach rumbled. It could be hunger. "What about your father?"

"He'll do anything to stay in my good books at the moment," he said, planting a kiss on each corner of her mouth. "I told him I was crazy about the devil's daughter. He said bring the little hussy to his retirement party next week."

"Will you protect me?" Her smile faded into pensiveness. "Wouldn't it be great if they could be friends one day?"

"They started that way," Nick said, nibbling his way around her jawline to her earlobe. "You'd be surprised at the impact a grandkid or two might have. It's our duty to work on improving relations between the two most stubborn old goats in New Zealand." He leaned back, his hands sliding from around her back to rest at the tops of her arms, holding her up. "To that end, Jordan Lake, would you marry me in the not-too-distant future? Any Friday will do."

Jordan caged his face with both hands, unable to stop a huge smile stretching her mouth wide. "Friday works for me." She leaned in and they touched foreheads, and stayed like that, smiling at each other, basking in a love that was sure to survive.

"Me, too," Nick murmured. "As long as I can have you every day in between."

Epilogue

The retirement party stepped up a notch once the formalities were dispensed with. It took Nick an age to get to the bar since everyone wanted to congratulate the new managing director along the way. He looked about for Jordan, thinking he'd barely seen her since the speeches. Randall had taken her under his wing and seemed determined to introduce her to every one of his cronies. With her tucked closely into his side, the old man practically dwarfed her slender form, in her striking, siren-red cocktail dress. He paraded her about proudly, as if she were *his* escort for the evening.

"Scotch, rocks," Nick said to the barman, and helped himself to an hors d'oeuvre from the platter on the bar. Jasmine had done an amazing job of organizing the retirement-cum-birthday-cum-promotion party on such short notice. Stunning floral arrangements and clusters of cheery balloons lifted the small former ballroom at the top of the Thorne building into an elegant venue, far removed from its normal function as a conference facility. The food and drink were top-notch, and the two hundred guests seemed to be enjoying themselves. Nick reminded himself to give his trusted personal assistant a decent bonus for her efforts.

"Well, big brother, it's your night, and not before time." Adam appeared out of the throng of people and saluted him with his glass. Nick reciprocated, and the brothers leaned with their backs to the bar, surveying the party.

"They look cozy," Adam commented, indicating their father and Jordan. "When are you going to let the best-kept secret out of the bag?"

Nick and Jordan's public relationship had sent the press into a frenzy, coming on the heels of the court case. Their expected engagement even had punters at the betting agency jostling for odds. "Soon," Nick replied. "I didn't want to steal Dad's thunder tonight."

"I suppose I'll have to come home for the wedding."

The happy couple wanted to get married as soon as possible, but Elenor confirmed that, even though he technically wasn't talking to them, her husband would expect the biggest and most flamboyant wedding ever staged in Wellington. They were doing their bit for family relations. It just wasn't possible to organize such a huge event before Adam left for England.

"You'll be back in the next few months, anyway."

Nick turned to Adam, but his brother wasn't listening. He was watching something or someone in the crowd. Nick followed his gaze and, sure enough, it was his personal assistant who held Adam's rapt attention.

Nick sighed. His brother hadn't taken his eyes off Jasmine all afternoon. Jordan had even commented on it. Hell, if he honestly thought Adam would ever settle down and take a woman seriously, Nick would be delighted in his choice. But Jasmine was too nice a person, and too valuable an employee, to have her heart broken by her boss's careless brother.

He took Adam's arm and turned him slightly. "I'd like to introduce you to a couple of our new corporate executives, Sandra and Melanie." He indicated two extremely attractive women in their twenties, deep in conversation by the punch bowl.

Adam didn't even look over. Jasmine had retreated to the corner of the room and slid her jacket off the back of a chair.

"I think I'll hit the road," Adam said, and drained his glass.

Nick laid a hand on his brother's arm. "Adam, you'll be gone in a day or so. Don't start anything with her."

Adam turned his light brown eyes on him. "I can give a woman a good time without breaking her heart, you know."

Nick knew there was little use in arguing once Adam's mind was made up. He was devilishly stubborn. Nonchalance might be a better weapon. "I'm only trying to keep you from making a fool of yourself. A woman like Jasmine wouldn't even give you the time of day. You're just not her type."

His brother only smiled, and giving him a look that clearly said, "Wanna bet?" Then he hightailed it toward the exit after the departing Jasmine.

Nick smelled Jordan's perfume and turned his head as a vision in red walked up to him. "I think your brother has just broken the hearts of every single female here by leaving," she quipped.

Nick gave her a rueful smile. "I should know by now that saying 'no can do' is like a red rag to a bull where Adam's concerned."

Jordan raised her brows.

Nick put his arms around her waist and pulled her in close. "Never mind. I have much more important things to think about. Such as—" he nuzzled her ear "—when can we leave?"

"Where are we going?" Jordan picked up his glass and stuck her nose into it, inhaling.

"I have a private function to attend at a certain hotel." Nick bumped their lower bodies together suggestively.

Grimacing at the smell of his Scotch, Jordan raised her eyes to his innocently. "I thought we were giving up the hotel on Fridays."

"Now why would we want to do that?"

"Because it's environmentally unfriendly, all that cleaning and polishing and lighting and so on."

Nick looked down into her shining eyes and beautiful smile, and silently thanked the Lord for cantankerous old men.

"And anyway," Jordan continued, "I spend half the week at your place and you spend the rest at mine."

"We're not married yet," Nick told his secret fiancée, "and until we are, you're my Friday mistress."

* * * * *

Celebrate 60 years of pure reading
pleasure with Harlequin®!
Silhouette® Romantic Suspense is celebrating with
the glamour-filled, adrenaline-charged series
LOVE IN 60 SECONDS
starting in April 2009.
Six stories that promise to bring the
glitz of Las Vegas, the danger of revenge,
the mystery of a missing diamond, family scandals
and ripped-from-the-headlines intrigue.
Get your heart racing as love happens
in sixty seconds!

Enjoy a sneak peek of
USA TODAY bestselling author Marie Ferrarella's
THE HEIRESS'S 2-WEEK AFFAIR
Available April 2009 from
Silhouette® Romantic Suspense.

Eight years ago Matt Shaffer had vanished out of Natalie Rothchild's life, leaving behind a one-line note tucked under a pillow that had grown cold: *I'm sorry, but this just isn't going to work.*

That was it. No explanation, no real indication of remorse. The note had been as clinical and compassionless as an eviction notice, which, in effect, it had been, Natalie thought as she navigated through the morning traffic. Matt had written the note to evict her from his life.

She'd spent the next two weeks crying, breaking down without warning as she walked down the street, or as she sat staring at a meal she couldn't bring herself to eat.

Candace, she remembered with a bittersweet pang,

had tried to get her to go clubbing in order to get her to forget about Matt.

She'd turned her twin down, but she did get her act together. If Matt didn't think enough of their relationship to try to contact her, to try to make her understand why he'd changed so radically from lover to stranger, then to hell with him. He was dead to her, she resolved. And he'd remained that way.

Until twenty minutes ago.

The adrenaline in her veins kept mounting.

Natalie focused on her driving. Vegas in the daylight wasn't nearly as alluring, as magical and glitzy as it was after dark. Like an aging woman best seen in soft lighting, Vegas's imperfections were all visible in the daylight. Natalie supposed that was why people like her sister didn't like to get up until noon. They lived for the night.

Except that Candace could no longer do that.

The thought brought a fresh, sharp ache with it.

"Damn it, Candy, what a waste," Natalie murmured under her breath.

She pulled up before the Janus casino. One of the three valets currently on duty came to life and made a beeline for her vehicle.

"Welcome to the Janus," the young attendant said cheerfully as he opened her door with a flourish.

"We'll see," she replied solemnly.

As he pulled away with her car, Natalie looked up at the casino's logo. Janus was the Roman god with two faces, one pointed toward the past, the other facing the future. It struck her as rather ironic, given what she was doing here, seeking out someone from her past in order to get answers so that the future could be settled.

The moment she entered the casino, the Vegas phenomena took hold. It was like stepping into a world where time did not matter or even make an appearance. There was only a sense of "now."

Because in Natalie's experience she'd discovered that bartenders knew the inner workings of any establishment they worked for better than anyone else, she made her way to the first bar she saw within the casino.

The bartender in attendance was a gregarious man in his early forties. He had a quick, sexy smile, which was probably one of the main reasons he'd been hired. His name tag identified him as Kevin.

Moving to her end of the bar, Kevin asked, "What'll it be, pretty lady?"

"Information." She saw a dubious look cross his brow. To counter that, she took out her badge. Granted she wasn't here in an official capacity, but Kevin didn't need to know that. "Were you on duty last night?"

Kevin began to wipe the gleaming black surface of the bar. "You mean during the gala?"

"Yes."

The smile gracing his lips was a satisfied one. Last night had obviously been profitable for him, she judged. "I caught an extra shift."

She took out Candace's photograph and carefully placed it on the bar. "Did you happen to see this woman there?"

The bartender glanced at the picture. Mild interest turned to recognition. "You mean Candace Rothchild? Yeah, she was here, loud and brassy as always. But not for long," he added, looking rather disappointed. There was always a circus when Candace was around, Natalie thought. "She and the boss had at it and then he had our head of security escort her out."

She latched onto the first part of his statement. "They argued? About what?"

He shook his head. "Couldn't tell you. Too far away for anything but body language," he confessed.

"And the head of security?" she asked.

"He got her to leave."

She leaned in over the bar. "Tell me about him."

"Don't know much," the bartender admitted. "Just that his name's Matt Shaffer. Boss flew him in from L.A., where he was head of security for Montgomery Enterprises."

There was no avoiding it, she thought darkly. She was going to have to talk to Matt. The thought left her cold. "Do you know where I can find him right now?"

Kevin glanced at his watch. "He should be in his office. On the second floor, toward the rear." He gave her the numbers of the rooms where the monitors that kept watch over the casino guests as they tried their luck against the house were located.

Taking out a twenty, she placed it on the bar. "Thanks for your help."

Kevin slipped the bill into his vest pocket. "Any time, lovely lady," he called after her. "Any time."

She debated going up the stairs, then decided on the elevator. The car that took her up to the second floor was empty. Natalie stepped out of the elevator, looked around to get her bearings and then walked toward the rear of the floor.

"Into the Valley of Death rode the six hundred," she silently recited, digging deep for a line from a poem by Tennyson. Wrapping her hand around a brass handle, she opened one of the glass doors and walked in.

The woman whose desk was closest to the door looked up. "You can't come in here. This is a restricted area."

Natalie already had her ID in her hand and held it up. "I'm looking for Matt Shaffer," she told the woman.

God, even saying his name made her mouth go dry. She was supposed to be over him, to have moved on with her life. What happened?

The woman began to answer her. "He's—"

"Right here."

The deep voice came from behind her. Natalie felt every single nerve ending go on tactical alert at the same moment that all the hairs at the back of her neck stood up. Eight years had passed, but she would have recognized his voice anywhere.

* * * * *

Why did Matt Shaffer leave heiress-turned-cop
Natalie Rothchild?
What does he know about the death of Natalie's
twin sister?
Come and meet these two reunited lovers and learn
the secrets of the Rothchild family in
THE HEIRESS'S 2-WEEK AFFAIR
by USA TODAY *bestselling author*
Marie Ferrarella.
The first book in Silhouette® Romantic Suspense's
wildly romantic new continuity,
LOVE IN 60 SECONDS!
Available April 2009.

CELEBRATE
60 YEARS
OF PURE READING PLEASURE
WITH HARLEQUIN®!

Look for Silhouette®
Romantic Suspense in April!

Love In 60 Seconds

Bright lights. Big city. Hearts in overdrive.

Silhouette® Romantic Suspense is celebrating
Harlequin's 60th Anniversary with six stories that
promise to bring readers the glitz of Las Vegas,
the danger of revenge, the mystery of a missing
diamond, and family scandals.

**Look for the first title, *The Heiress's 2-Week Affair*
by *USA TODAY* bestselling author
Marie Ferrarella, on sale in April!**

His 7-Day Fiancée by **Gail Barrett**	May
The 9-Month Bodyguard by **Cindy Dees**	June
Prince Charming for 1 Night by **Nina Bruhns**	July
Her 24-Hour Protector by **Loreth Anne White**	August
5 minutes to Marriage by **Carla Cassidy**	September

REQUEST YOUR FREE BOOKS!

2 FREE NOVELS PLUS 2 FREE GIFTS!

Passionate, Powerful, Provocative!

YES! Please send me 2 FREE Silhouette Desire® novels and my 2 FREE gifts (gifts are worth about $10). After receiving them, if I don't wish to receive any more books, I can return the shipping statement marked "cancel". If I don't cancel, I will receive 6 brand-new novels every month and be billed just $4.05 per book in the U.S. or $4.74 per book in Canada, plus 25¢ shipping and handling per book and applicable taxes, if any*. That's a savings of almost 15% off the cover price! I understand that accepting the 2 free books and gifts places me under no obligation to buy anything. I can always return a shipment and cancel at any time. Even if I never buy another book, the two free books and gifts are mine to keep forever.

225 SDN ERVX 326 SDN ERVM

Name	(PLEASE PRINT)	
Address		Apt. #
City	State/Prov.	Zip/Postal Code

Signature (if under 18, a parent or guardian must sign)

Mail to the **Silhouette Reader Service:**
IN U.S.A.: P.O. Box 1867, Buffalo, NY 14240-1867
IN CANADA: P.O. Box 609, Fort Erie, Ontario L2A 5X3

Not valid to current subscribers of Silhouette Desire books.

Want to try two free books from another line?
Call 1-800-873-8635 or visit www.morefreebooks.com.

* Terms and prices subject to change without notice. N.Y. residents add applicable sales tax. Canadian residents will be charged applicable provincial taxes and GST. Offer not valid in Quebec. This offer is limited to one order per household. All orders subject to approval. Credit or debit balances in a customer's account(s) may be offset by any other outstanding balance owed by or to the customer. Please allow 4 to 6 weeks for delivery. Offer available while quantities last.

Your Privacy: Silhouette Books is committed to protecting your privacy. Our Privacy Policy is available online at www.eHarlequin.com or upon request from the Reader Service. From time to time we make our lists of customers available to reputable third parties who may have a product or service of interest to you. If you would prefer we not share your name and address, please check here. ☐

SDES08R

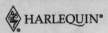

THE RAKE'S INHERITED COURTESAN
Ann Lethbridge

Christopher Evernden has been
assigned the unfortunate task of minding
Parisian courtesan Sylvia Boisette.
When Syliva sets off to find her father,
Christopher has no choice but to follow
and finds her kidnapped by an Irishman.
Once rescued, they finally succumb to
the temptation that has been brewing
between them. But can they see past the
limitations such a love can bring?

Available April 2009
wherever books are sold.

COMING NEXT MONTH
Available April 14, 2009

#1933 THE UNTAMED SHEIK—Tessa Radley
Man of the Month
Whisking a suspected temptress to his desert palace seems the only way to stop her…until unexpected attraction flares and he discovers she may not be what he thought after all.

#1934 BARGAINED INTO HER BOSS'S BED—Emilie Rose
The Hudsons of Beverly Hills
He'll do anything to get what he wants—including seduce his assistant to keep her from quitting!

#1935 THE MORETTI SEDUCTION—Katherine Garbera
Moretti's Legacy
This charming tycoon has never heard the word *no*—until now. Attracted to his business rival, he finds himself in a fierce battle both in the boardroom…and the bedroom.

#1936 DAKOTA DADDY—Sara Orwig
Stetsons & CEOs
Determined to buy a ranch from his former lover and family rival, he's shocked to discover he's a father! Now he'll stop at nothing short of seduction to get his son.

#1937 PRETEND MISTRESS, BONA FIDE BOSS—
Yvonne Lindsay
Rogue Diamonds
His plan had been to proposition his secretary into being his companion for the weekend. But he *didn't* plan on wanting more than just a business relationship….

#1938 THE HEIR'S SCANDALOUS AFFAIR—
Jennifer Lewis
The Hardcastle Progeny
When the mysterious woman he spent a passionate night with returns to tell him he may be a Hardcastle, he wonders what a Hardcastle man should do to get her back in his bed.

SDCNMBPA0309